Annie smiled  **him. 'You're Toby attitude care more abo**

He sighed. 'Being a parent does that to you. It makes you think more clearly, realise the consequences of your actions. But I'm still the same Toby underneath.'

To prove it, he smiled the old Toby smile. 'Bye, Annie. I'll not see you till late tonight, but we'll make more arrangements tomorrow. I'm taking Charlie to Jack's for a couple of hours. So the family can get to know their nephew.' And he was gone.

Annie sighed when he had left. 'Realise the consequences of your actions, indeed.' He had a few more lessons to learn. But what an awful lot *she* had learned about Toby Sinclair in the past few days. And she realised that what she had learned had made her love him more than ever.

Dear Reader

A year ago I wrote three books—A VERY SPECIAL MIDWIFE, A CHILD TO CALL HER OWN, and THE NOBLE DOCTOR. They were about life in a maternity unit in a large city hospital, the Dell Owen. I was really pleased at the number of letters I received, saying how much readers had enjoyed the Dell Owen trilogy, and asking was there any chance of any more? No need to ask; I love writing about maternity. So now we have another three.

My daughter is a midwife. She supplies me with the technical details for my stories, and the feelings that nurses, doctors, midwives have about their profession. They are trained not to let their feelings show— but they are there, especially in a life-enhancing department like Maternity.

These three books are about two brothers and a sister, all working together in the Dell Owen Hospital. Jack, Toby and Carly are vastly different in character, united in their love for each other, but feel that sibling rivalry that is a part of so many high-achieving families. All three fall in love—though *the course of true love never did run smooth'*.

I hope you get as much pleasure from reading about the Dell Owen Hospital staff as I get from writing about them. **Look out for Carly's story, coming soon in Mills & Boon® Medical Romance™.**

With all good wishes

Gill Sanderson

THE DOCTOR'S BABY SURPRISE

BY

GILL SANDERSON

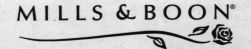

MILLS & BOON®

All the characters in this book have no existence outside the imagination
of the author, and have no relation whatsoever to anyone bearing the
same name or names. They are not even distantly inspired by any
individual known or unknown to the author, and all the incidents are
pure invention.

First published in Great Britain 2006
Paperback edition 2007
Harlequin Mills & Boon Limited,
Eton House, 18-24 Paradise Road, Richmond, Surrey TW9 1SR

© Gill Sanderson 2006

ISBN-13: 978 0 263 85222 6
ISBN-10:   0 263 85222 9

Set in Times Roman 10½ on 12¾ pt
03-0207-45728

Printed and bound in Spain
by Litografia Rosés, S.A., Barcelona

Gill Sanderson, aka Roger Sanderson, started writing as a husband-and-wife team. At first Gill created the storyline, characters and background, asking Roger to help with the actual writing. But her job became more and more time-consuming and he took over all of the work. He loves it!

Roger has written many Medical Romance™ books for Harlequin Mills & Boon®. Ideas come from three of his children—Helen is a midwife, Adam a health visitor, Mark a consultant oncologist. Week days are for work; weekends find Roger walking in the Lake District or Wales.

Recent titles by the same author:

A SURGEON, A MIDWIFE: A FAMILY*
A NURSE WORTH WAITING FOR
TELL ME YOU LOVE ME
THE NOBLE DOCTOR*
A CHILD TO CALL HER OWN*
A VERY SPECIAL MIDWIFE*

Dell Owen Maternity

For Fin Walsh—Many happy days

CHAPTER ONE

THE nurse held the baby, gently but firmly, on her side. Annie had cleansed the tiny back and injected lignocaine, a local anaesthetic. Now she found the space between vertebrae four and five, positioned the needle. A quick glance upwards at Jack Sinclair, the neonate surgeon. He nodded. Annie pushed in the needle.

Baby Matilda had a possible central nervous disorder—meningitis was suspected. The quickest way to diagnose was by taking some cerebrospinal fluid.

It was important not to push the needle in too far, and Annie checked frequently to see there was no blood in the specimen. But eventually she was able to obtain her few drops of fluid and transfer them safely into the specimen bottles. She withdrew the needle and pressure was kept over the area until no more CSF appeared. Then a spray dressing was applied. The specimens were dispatched straight to the lab and Annie's job was done.

She had finished for the day now, and Jack had work somewhere else. But for a minute they had time to sit in the doctors' room, drinking coffee out of plastic cups.

'Your first neonatal lumbar puncture,' Jack said with a smile. 'How did it feel?'

She thought about it, her emotions still mixed. 'I was nervous at first, but then I think I got into the swing of it. Once I saw that I was doing it right, it felt easier.'

'Good. You did a competent job. Would you be happy to do it again on your own?'

There was no doubt about the answer to this. 'Yes. It wasn't all that different to doing a puncture on an adult.'

'Only a question of size. The innards are all the same—just smaller.'

She nodded. 'That's it. Smaller. I can work on adults with no problems at all. But cutting or sticking needles in babies as tiny as these, when they're newborn and they seem so perfect—it still seems a bit unfair.'

'Just think of the consequences if we didn't stick needles or cut,' he advised her. 'And think of our success rate compared with even a dozen years ago.'

'I do think of it. It's one reason why I thought of training to be a neonatal surgeon.'

Jack nodded. 'You're still happy now you've changed your mind? You still want to specialise in O and G? You've worked with me; I think you could have the makings of a very good surgeon.'

She had thought for hours about this decision but had finally made up her mind. 'I think I'm happiest with O and G.'

He laughed. 'A good reason. Now, let's move from professional to personal. You are coming to our engagement party tonight?'

She saw the hesitancy in his eyes and realised he was worried that she wouldn't come. When she didn't reply at once he went on, 'I want you there, I really do. That is both of us, both me and Miranda, we want you there. We want you to be happy for us.'

Her voice was cheerful—genuinely cheerful. 'Jack, nothing would keep me away from your engagement party. I feel I did my bit in bringing you two together, and I want to celebrate that.'

She could joke about it now, and she eyed him wryly. 'You're worried about how I'll react when I see your brother, aren't you? You're worried that I won't be able to cope.'

She saw the hesitancy in his eyes again and reached over to touch his hand, to reassure him. 'Jack, it's all over now. Perhaps there was something between us but now it's over and Toby and I can be friends. I'm sure we can work together and get on. It'll be fine, I'm certain of it.'

Reassured, Jack smiled. 'I'm glad. Like you said, you helped in bringing me together with Miranda, and I'll always be grateful.'

He glanced at the clock on the wall. 'Time I was moving. See you tonight, then.'

And he strode away.

Annie smiled to herself, wondering if he entirely believed what she had just said. But he had no need to worry. Whatever there was—whatever there had been—between her and Toby Sinclair was now dead. She was over him, could look forward to a new life, perhaps find a new love. And she had just done her first neonatal lumbar puncture!

Everything was right in her world. Annie drove to her flat thinking that the future held nothing but good for her. She was established in her profession, and in eighteen months' time she would no longer be an SHO but could apply to be a junior registrar. She wanted to specialise in O and G. She thought she was doing well at the work. Her friend was getting married. And she was over her affair with Toby Sinclair. He was nothing to her now. Who was to tell? Perhaps soon, perhaps even this evening, she might meet the man who was the one for her.

But it had been a long day and it was going to be a longer evening. She seized the rare chance and relaxed for half an hour.

She sat in her flat, eyes closed, feet stretched along the couch, a mug of tea in her hand. The flat was quiet, her flatmate Miranda now spending most of her time at Jack's flat. Annie had quite enjoyed living with Miranda. They had gossiped, talked about Miranda's on-off relationship with Jack. Annie thought about it. Seeing Miranda find love and happiness after the most doubtful of beginnings—it made her feel that perhaps she too could find an equally special relationship. There must be a chance for her somewhere!

Perhaps inevitably she started to think about Toby Sinclair, Jack's younger brother, like her an SHO but in his second year. She only thought of him because, well…he had been the man she had been most involved with. No feelings for him now, of course. She was just indulging herself. What he had done to her had been awful.

A quick vision of him flashed before her eyes and she had to admit he was gorgeous. It wasn't just that he was tall and broad-shouldered. Or that his hair was slightly too long and sometimes flopped over his face. Or even his clothes—Toby liked to look good and he certainly did.

It was odd, because although Toby was a very skilful and dedicated doctor, people remembered him because of his smile. It showed that he felt that everyone was his friend. And everyone was! Toby loved people and showed it.

The trouble came when they started loving him back. As she had started to love him back.

But now the agony was over. For a while it had hurt—had hurt desperately. It had even hurt that she'd had to hide from him just how much he had hurt her. But she had her pride. And now the hurt had gone.

She was over Toby Sinclair, had made herself get over him. She remembered the light-hearted 'good, bad and ugly' nicknames given to the three Sinclair siblings by hospital staff, with sweet-natured Carly the good, playboy Toby the bad and Jack, with his craggy yet compelling face, the ugly. Toby had definitely been bad, but not for her any more. Now she had so much more to look forward to. She was pressing on with her life and it showed so much promise.

* * *

She had bought new clothes for this party, it was going to be a party to remember. After a long luxurious soak in the bath she slipped into her new underwear. New underwear always made her feel special. For a while she sat at her dressing table in her tiny scraps of pink silk and dried her shoulder-length dark curls. Then she dressed in a bias-cut black skirt and a new scarlet silk top.

A touch of make-up followed. Lipstick, mascara, a smear of moisturiser. She looked at herself approvingly in the mirror. Yes, she looked good. Then, last of all, a dab of scent on her wrists, behind her ears, in her cleavage. Having never really bothered with perfume before, she had bought this particular scent deliberately, after her split with Toby. It was to mark her moving back into the real world, a self-assured, attractive young woman who was ready to meet any man—but on her terms.

She phoned for a taxi. Tonight she might have more than the two small drinks which were her strict ration when she was driving. As she picked up the engagement present for Miranda and Jack, she wondered how the evening would turn out. Might she meet the man who could make her as happy as Jack made Miranda happy? No matter, in time he would turn up. There must be some good men somewhere. Not all were like Toby Sinclair.

There was a feeling of excitement in the hospital social club. Or perhaps it she was who was excited. This was a good day for her! She dropped off her coat and was shown to a large, cheerfully decorated room. There was a banner with MIRANDA and JACK printed on it, the words surrounded with a border of interlinked hearts. There was a bar, a buffet being set out and a band warming up. Only a few guests were there. Annie had deliberately come early as she wanted to talk to Miranda before she became too busy.

Miranda was sitting down—her recent operation meant that she still had to take things very carefully. Annie walked over, kissed her friend on the cheek and offered her a box, skilfully wrapped in silver paper. 'Congratulations, honey. If you hadn't picked Jack, I'd have had him myself.'

Miranda grinned at her friend. 'Annie! You look absolutely fabulous. I'm so glad you could come. What's this?'

'Engagement present. When you get married you can have something worthy and boring, like cutlery or bedsheets. But getting engaged—something frivolous.'

'Jack! Come over here. Annie says she's bought us something frivolous.'

Jack was standing near the bar. He turned when Miranda called him and then smiled happily when he saw Annie. 'Something frivolous?' he asked as he walked over to join them. 'My serious and dedicated SHO—buying something frivolous?' He gave her a kiss on the cheek. 'Annie, it's so good to see you.'

'Open it,' Miranda said, thrusting the box towards Jack. 'I want to see what's inside.'

Annie watched apprehensively as Jack ripped away the silver covering, opened the box inside and from the masses of tissue paper took out a large engraved glass with two handles. It was always hard, choosing a present that fitted an occasion perfectly.

'It's a loving cup,' she said. 'It symbolises your to-getherness. If you have a banquet you're supposed to drink out of it alternately.'

Miranda's eyes filled with tears. 'It's lovely, Annie. I'll have it on the table when we get married. It'll be the first thing we drink out of.'

Jack stooped and kissed his future wife's cheek before smiling at Annie. 'Might have expected something like this from you,' he said. 'I think it's lovely, too.'

Miranda flapped her hand at him. 'Go and put this on the table with the other presents. Make sure it goes at the front. I want just a five-minute chat with Annie before the party starts properly.'

Jack winked at Annie. 'Starting as we intend to go on,' he said. 'Miranda orders, I obey. We'll have a talk later.'

Annie looked at the way he smiled down at Miranda, caught the expression on Miranda's face and, for a moment, felt envious. She wanted someone to look at her like that. Still…plenty of time.

'Oh, Miranda, before I forget, I wanted to talk to you about the flat,' she said. 'We both know you'll never come back to the flat. And although you've said you want to, I'm not having you paying half of the rent. So I've found someone else to move in.'

'Someone I know?' Miranda was curious.

'He's called Calvin Winterson, he's a friend of Carly's from Chicago. Joining the infectious diseases department for six months.'

Miranda grinned wickedly. 'A man!'

Annie laughed, shaking her head. 'He's fifteen years older than me and married. His wife is in London. He loves her dearly and will go down to London every weekend to see her. Sorry to disappoint you!'

'Well, he sounds OK,' Miranda said thoughtfully. 'You're sure you'll be all—'

'I'm certain. Calvin is perfect.' She grinned. 'Calvin will be peaceful. He won't be filling the flat with handsome young men when I'm trying to get changed. In fact, I suspect I'll hardly ever see him. But, anyway, have you decided on the wedding date yet? And do I get to be a bridesmaid? And most important, if I am a bridesmaid, can I choose my own dress?'

Then, for a split second, the world stopped.

Of course she had known it would happen, was expecting it. But, still, there was that little thrill of disturbance when she saw him for the first time. As Miranda talked dresses, Annie saw Toby walking into the room with a couple of his friends. Typically, he looked wonderful. He was wearing a dark grey suit, the jacket slung casually over his shoulder. His shirt was expensive, by a well-known designer—she remembered it so well because he had been wearing it the first time that they… Did he have to wear it today when he knew that…? Annoyed, Annie pulled herself together. She was being stupid! What was a shirt?

Miranda had felt her friend stiffen. In an elaborately casual voice she said, 'Oh, look, there's Toby.'

'So it is.' Annie turned to face her friend and, smiled. 'Miranda, don't worry, all that Toby business is over.'

Miranda wasn't convinced. 'Are you really sure?'

'Of course I'm sure. I'm a bright twenty-five-year-old doctor with my future in front of me. I was a bit upset at first—but I'm not going to ruin my life because of one small mistake.'

Do you see much of him?'

Annie shrugged. 'We don't try to avoid each other but we don't seek out each other's company either. We're just doctors who sometimes work in the same department.'

'Good, I'm glad. I want you to be happy. And I know Jack's been worried. He thinks a lot of you, partly because you're a good worker and partly because you're my closest friend. And then he loves his brother—even though they're vastly different in character.'

Annie was curious. 'Do they see much of each other outside the hospital?'

'Apparently more than they used to, say, a couple of years ago. But Jack says Toby is different—as if he has his own demons he can't deal with.'

'Well, it's not me. He dealt with me very fairly— I suppose.'

'Perhaps just the work getting on top of him. Jack rides him pretty hard.'

Annie shook her head. 'It's not that. Jack rides us all hard, which is why we like him. Well, Toby will have to find his own salvation.' They both looked at Toby, now the centre of a group of laughing friends. 'He doesn't look very worried now,' she said.

The room was filling up now and people were making their way over to Miranda. Annie knew she shouldn't monopolise her friend, so she touched her gently on the shoulder and said, 'You've got to greet your guests so I'm going to circulate a bit. We'll have another talk later.' Then she walked away.

Annie walked to the bar and was offered a glass of champagne. She took it then moved to a shadowed corner of the room. She knew practically everyone there so she would have no difficulty in finding a group to stand with, to chat to. But for the moment she thought she'd like just to stand and observe.

Inevitably, she looked at Toby. In some way he was the most outstanding man in the room. It wasn't just his size, the fact that he looked—she had to admit—gorgeous. It was because he seemed always to be smiling. Annie watched as he wandered through the crowd, noticed how many people seemed genuinely pleased to see him. She noticed that he spent as much time chatting to an elderly member of the cleaning staff as he did talking to senior members of the department who could influence his future career.

Vaguely she wondered just how useful a happy smile or happy personality could be to a practising doctor. He made all his patients feel that he was their friend, that he loved them. In fact, that had been the first thing that had…

Stop it! They'd had their fling, they had parted. She was not to think about him any more. And now she had to look forward to her future. A future without Toby. She knew she could do it. Though it would be hard.

And now it was time to join the party and be happy for her friends.

Toby took a mouthful of champagne and wondered if he was getting old. He didn't seem to have the same delight in parties as he used to have. Of course, this was a good party. He was happy for his brother, even, perhaps, slightly envious. Jack's joy was obvious for everyone to see. Toby wondered how long it had been since he had felt so joyful.

Still, this was a good party. There were old friends to catch up with, perhaps new friends to meet... He looked round the now filling room. And saw Annie Arnold.

She had her back to him, she was wearing clothes that he hadn't seen before but he recognised her at once. As he looked, she half turned to speak to someone and he caught his breath as he saw her smile and reacted to that unconscious, casually provocative pose, his gaze captured by the delicious curve of her figure and her silky dark hair.

He sighed and for a moment wondered what he had given up. He hadn't seen much of her recently and she seemed to have changed. Was her face thinner? When she wasn't smiling it made her look wistful—sad even. He didn't like to think of her sad.

He moved to one side so he could look at her more fully, lifted his glass so no one would know what he was doing. Perhaps her face wasn't more sad, perhaps it was his imagination. He knew he had hurt her—but it was all for her ultimate good. Pity she couldn't know that.

He wrenched his gaze away, turned to look for friends, acquaintances. This was supposed to be a party. An occasion for joy!

And he did enjoy himself, talking to people and generally having a good time. But then, as he turned away from one small group, he met her, face to face. She couldn't be avoided. He saw the slight shock of recognition on her face, the wariness that followed. He wondered what his own face told her.

But she seemed entirely unperturbed. 'Hello, Toby, good to see you. Great party, isn't it?'

'Wonderful,' he agreed. 'I think my brother has done really well for himself. I'm envious.'

Then he wondered if that had been an entirely sensitive thing to say.

But Annie didn't seem to mind. 'Plenty of other women around,' she said lightly. 'You can still go on looking.'

This was the kind of dialogue he could manage easily. 'No matter how hard I look, I'll not find another Miranda. But any woman who can dominate big brother Jack—she is really something.'

Annie smiled at his teasing tone. 'She doesn't dominate him. She loves him and because of that he wants to make her happy.'

'Sounds like domination to me. Only it's cunning domination.'

So, a light, pointless, teasing conversation. But his

thoughts were very different. Yes, perhaps her face was a touch thinner but it was as lovely as ever. And the rest of her—that scarlet top had every man trying not to stare at it. What it didn't reveal it suggested.

An emotion he couldn't identify jerked through him. Regret…sadness…guilt…he just didn't know. Perhaps some combination of all of these. A vague feeling of loss, of what might have been but couldn't be.

He didn't like being in doubt. So he hunched his shoulders and did what he always did—met any problem head on. Not that Annie was a problem but… 'Would you like to dance?' he asked. This one's nice and slow.'

'Dance with you? For old times' sake?'

'No. Because I want to dance with you and you're the best-looking girl in the room.'

'That's the Toby we all know and love,' she said, slightly mocking. 'How many girls will you say that to tonight?'

'I meant it,' he protested cheerfully. 'You're the best-looking girl in the room.' He paused a moment and then went on, 'Apart from Miranda, that is. She just has to be the best looking, this is her party.'

Both of them turned to look at Miranda. 'I think my brother is very lucky,' Toby said, suddenly sounding very serious. 'She's gorgeous.'

Annie nodded. 'So she is. And I think she's very lucky, too, having Jack. Now, are we going to dance or stand here and talk about it?'

He was a little surprised at that, but took her hand and led her onto the dance floor. Then he slipped his arm round her waist. There was an odd pang as he felt the warmth and softness of her body.

They moved gently to the music and for once in his life he wasn't sure what to say. But there was something. 'You're wearing perfume,' he said. 'That's something new, you never used to. But I like it.'

'It's part of my new image,' she said simply. 'A lot has changed about me and wearing perfume is an example.'

He didn't know what to reply. For a while they moved easily to the music, perfectly attuned, her body knowing just what his was doing, responding instinctively. They moved well together. He was enjoying himself more than he could have imagined. But there was something missing between them.

Go for it. Risk the consequences, say what he thought.

'I, er…hope you don't still feel bad about our parting,' he said. 'I'd hate it if there was any ill feeling between us.'

She smiled. 'We didn't part,' she said. 'Parting suggests some kind of a joint decision. You dumped me. I'm sure it was for the very best of reasons, but no girl likes being dumped. Still, I'm well over it now. I really am.'

Toby was having difficulty coping with this. 'Well over it,' he mumbled. 'Good, I wouldn't want to hurt you. So I'm forgiven?'

It looked as if she had to think about this. Then, 'Yes, you're forgiven. Forgiven if not forgotten. You are you and everyone loves you the way you are. Which lucky girl are you taking home tonight?'

For some reason that didn't please him. 'You said we

were dancing for old times' sake.' He managed a cheeky grin, trying to keep it light-hearted. 'Could I take you home for old times' sake?'

Annie laughed. 'I've been one notch on your bedpost already. I'm not going to let you make it a double notch.'

'Ouch,' said Toby. 'That hurt.'

'The truth often does hurt.'

He smiled at that, he had to, it was his way. But it did hurt. He supposed his reputation was deserved and in some ways he had cultivated it. Everyone knew what he was like. And that was the way he needed to be.

The music was coming to an end. He sketched her an elaborate bow and asked, 'Would Mademoiselle like another dance?'

She shook her head. 'Perhaps later. But for now there are a lot of friends I have to catch up with. Thanks for the dance, Toby. I'd forgotten how well we fitted together.' And she walked away.

Toby accepted that what she had said was very reasonable. But it didn't stop a heavy weight settling in his chest as he watched her departing back.

He decided that the best thing was to go to get another drink. Then he danced with some very pretty nurses, all of whom seemed eager to get to know him better. But for some reason he just wasn't interested. All he could remember was what Annie had asked him. *Which lucky girl are you taking home tonight?* He knew it had been half joke, half bitter comment. And suddenly, even though he was enjoying the company of his current dance partner, a beautiful theatre nurse who was currently twining her arms around his neck, he didn't want her to be the girl he took home.

Tactfully he extricated himself and moved on. Time to speak to his sister-in-law-to-be. He saw that, just for a moment, Miranda was on her own and went up to her, giving her an affectionate kiss on the cheek.

'Hey, gorgeous.' He grinned. 'So you're marrying my brother Jack. I don't know if that is a cause for congratulations or commiserations, but I'm happy for both of you and so welcome to the family. As you know, every family has to have a black sheep and it looks like I'm the one.'

'Sheep can be sheared,' Miranda pointed out. 'Even you.'

Toby ran his hand over his thick dark hair. 'A dreadful thought.' He stooped to kiss her again then handed her a gold-coloured envelope. 'This is an engagement present. Hope you like it.'

Miranda eyed him thoughtfully. 'Am I going to get a shock when I open this?' she asked. 'I know it's not a frying-pan, the envelope's too small.' She opened the envelope. A congratulations card, of course, and attached to it a gift card for a relaxing break for two in a luxury hotel. Miranda smiled. 'Toby, that's a fantastic idea. Thank you so much!' She stood, flung her arms round his neck and kissed him.

'Thought it might be nice for you two to get away for a bit. We Sinclairs try to please,' said Toby urbanely.

Miranda put the gold envelope in her handbag and

looked assessingly at him. 'I saw you dancing with Annie,' she said. 'You looked very happy together.'

His expression gave nothing away. 'We're old friends. We had something going—it's over now.'

'Whatever you say. But when are you going to provide me with another sister-in-law? There must be the right woman for you somewhere.'

He smiled easily. 'I've looked hard enough.'

'Yes, we've noticed. And have you never found anyone who was the right person for you?'

Then he made one of his rare mistakes. 'Found the right person for me?' he said. 'Once I did and then I found out that nothing is for ever so I...' Then he blinked.

He was enjoying the party, he had had one glass of champagne and two of red wine. Before that he'd worked an over-long and very hard shift. Perhaps he was more tired than he knew. Certainly he was more careless.

He could feel Miranda looking at him, thoughtfully, expectantly. 'Nothing is for ever? Tell me more.'

Time to concentrate! Move back into cheerful Toby mode. 'I met the love of my life,' he said lightly. 'But then I discovered that her father wasn't rich enough. So she had to go.'

'You're a tease,' Miranda complained. 'There's good sense in you but I can never get at it.'

'Miranda, congratulations!'

Both Miranda and Toby looked up, to see three of the consultants from neighbouring wards. They'd just arrived. 'Talk to you later,' Toby whispered, and slipped away.

For a moment he stood in the shadowed side of the

room, bit his lip and breathed a small prayer, asking for forgiveness. Then he smiled and moved back to join his group of friends.

It had been a good party, Annie decided. She had enjoyed herself. She lay in her bath, gently splashing water over her body and thought about the highlights. She had talked with old friends, she had enjoyed a superb buffet, she had—shame on her—drunk enough champagne to make her quite certain that she had been right not to have come in her own car. Both Miranda and Jack had made short speeches. She had enjoyed those, too. But most of all she was happy because she knew that she was finally and absolutely over Toby.

She knew that her friends had been conspiring to keep them apart. Now it just wasn't necessary. They could work together, perhaps even be friends. She knew that he had no idea—*could* have no idea—just how much he had hurt her. And she was not going to inflict that on him.

It had been hard for a while but she had survived. Now she should be focusing on the future.

But he *had* looked good.

CHAPTER TWO

A SENIOR house officer was certainly a doctor. She could call herself Dr Arnold, was licensed to prescribe drugs, could conduct examinations. But being an SHO wasn't always at the fascinating, cutting edge of medicine. In the middle of the next morning Annie found herself sitting in the doctors' room, filling in forms. She knew that records were an essential part of medicine. But they were boring!

The door opened behind her and a male voice said, 'It's good to see someone working.'

Slightly surprised, she turned, but she'd recognised that voice at once. Toby. Still, why not? He was as entitled to be there as she was.

'What are you doing?' he asked. A casual question, one doctor to another.

'Drugs records. Apparently we now have to satisfy the accountants as well as the consultants.'

He winced. 'Modern medicine, cash led. As your doctor I prescribe an instant infusion of coffee. May I get you a mug?'

'Please. You know how I like it.' Then she, too, winced. That had been a mistake.

But he fetched her coffee without comment. This was all a bit new. For quite a while—well, since their break-up—if he walked into a room where she was standing he would casually walk out again. If she saw him she would avoid him. There was nothing too obvious but it was there. And she knew that their friends had tried—again without being too obvious—to keep them apart.

But now it was good to know that there was no need. Everything was over and they were back to being just colleagues.

'Great party,' she said. 'I really enjoyed it.'

'Me, too. Good to see two people so happy. It was enough to make someone think that they ought to get engaged as well. Don't you think so?'

She pursed her lips. 'Not really. You've got to find the right man and the right woman.'

'And they're hard to find and to put together?'

'It's almost impossible.'

He sighed and shook his head. 'It's a sad situation when we can't rely on women to be romantic. See you, Annie.' He carried his coffee out of the room.

Annie nodded to herself when he had gone. She was OK with him now. She could get on with her boring paperwork. But two minutes later her pager sounded. She checked it, rang John Bennett, her head of department. 'Got a minute to drop in and see me?' he asked.

* * *

John Bennett searched through the papers on his very cluttered desk, found one, glanced at it and said, 'You enjoy working in Obs and Gynae.'

It was a statement rather than a question. 'Yes, I do. I would like—I hope—to specialise in it.'

'So you'll want to do another six months rotation with us?'

'If you'll have me.'

John looked at the paper in his hand again, nodding thoughtfully. 'I think so. People seem pleased with your work. Your logbook is up to date? You're working towards your Part One of the MRCOG exam?'

'My logbook is fine and I'm studying for the exam.'

Passing Part One of the Medical Research Council Obstetrics and Gynaecology examination was the first step towards Annie's dream of being an accredited O and G consultant.

'Good,' John said. 'Now, you know the job of an SHO is generally to make sure that everything goes smoothly for those higher up the ladder? Be a general dogsbody?'

'I know the work has to be done.' Annie was cautious.

'So it has. But we're going to give you just a little more responsibility, promote you a bit. We're opening a new clinic, delivery and postnatal, and I want you to help run it. It will operate on three days a week. That'll give you time to fulfill your other obligations and attend your SHO teaching sessions. It will specialise in those cases that the district midwife thinks needs extra medical care and will also often mean you assisting in difficult deliveries. There'll be home visits, too.'

'I'd like that,' Annie said. 'I'd like that very much.' Secretly she was delighted, but she didn't know whether to show it or not.

'It'll be hard work but you'll learn a lot. And in some ways it'll be more rewarding. You'll have more time to get to know your patients. They'll become people instead of just women passing through.' John put down the paper, stared at her. 'There'll be the usual chain of command above you—registrars, a consultant eventually—but I anticipate much of the work being done by two SHOs. You and one who has done one six-month rotation already. The senior SHO will be Toby Sinclair.' He paused. 'I know you two have some history so I wanted to ask you now if you would be happy to work with him.'

'Absolutely no problem,' Annie said confidently. 'I'd like to work with Toby.' She smiled and went on, 'Did you ask him if he was happy to work with me?'

'I did.' Annie could see that John was choosing his words carefully as he went on. 'And he said that there's no SHO in the hospital that he'd rather work with.'

'That's very gratifying. I hope your confidence in us both is justified. Now, when do we start?'

'Next Monday,' John said. 'And good luck.'

Annie went back to her dreary paperwork feeling rather pleased with life. This was promotion, of a sort. Well, at least recognition of her good work so far. Working in the clinic would be a change; she'd learn a lot. And Toby was ahead of her; she would learn from working with him.

And she was getting on fine with Toby now, wasn't she?

Toby hesitated outside the doctors' room, wondering exactly how to put things. He'd just been told that he was going to work at the new clinic with Annie. He'd just been told that she was looking forward to working with him. This pleased him—but puzzled him at the same time.

Fortunately there was only Annie in the doctors' room. She was bent over her paperwork again and looked up as he entered. 'I've just heard that we're going to be working together,' he said. 'Are you really OK with that?'

He was relieved if a little surprised when she said, 'Of course I'm looking forward to working with you. Why shouldn't I be OK with that?'

That rather confused him. 'Well,' he mumbled, 'things between us have been…'

She laughed. 'Toby! We had a fling and now I'm over it, OK? I hope you're not going to drag this up every time we meet.'

'Well, no,' he said. He supposed he ought to be quite pleased. He wandered round the doctors' room, picking up magazines, squinting at notices, for some reason unable to sit down and have the five minutes' rest he so desperately needed.

'In a sense we've both been promoted,' Annie went on. 'Isn't that a good thing?'

After a while Toby nodded. 'I suppose so. So we are going to get on with each other?'

'We are. I'll learn from you, Toby, which is why I'm looking forward to working with you. You always pull your weight. You've got a year's more experience than me. I can rely on you for advice.' She grinned at him. 'You can be my big brother.'

Toby frowned. 'Are you sure you want me to be your big brother?' he asked. 'Big brothers can be an interfering nuisance.'

'Is Jack an interfering nuisance, then? I wouldn't have thought so.'

Toby obviously felt he had to be fair. 'No. I guess Jack isn't a nuisance. But he certainly feels that he's entitled to make his views known.'

'Then you can make your views known to me.'

'Just on medical matters?'

'Well, what else have we got in common?' she asked lightly. 'Now, back to paperwork.' She bent her head over the files in front of her. Toby sighed and, without much success, tried to read a magazine.

There was silence for five minutes. Then from behind him there came the sound of a hand slapping a pile of papers and a satisfied voice saying, 'Done!' He turned to watch Annie stuffing sheaves of paper into her briefcase. 'I've finished the paperwork and I'm an hour ahead of myself,' she said happily.

Toby hesitated before speaking. 'Annie, we're going to be working together. If you've got a few minutes to spare, you might like to wander round the gynae ward with me. We can get used to each other's ways of working. I've got just a few things to check and then I'm doing an exchange transfusion. Want to help?'

'I'd love to,' Annie said.

It was interesting, working so closely with him. At first his closeness bothered her a little. When they leaned together over an incubator, sometimes she could feel the warmth of his breath. His arms brushed against hers. Their fingers touched when he handed her a sheaf of notes. There was that tingle that she remembered—but, of course, all that was in the past. Now they were colleagues. And he was both a good doctor and a good teacher.

Both leaned over a premature baby, listened to her heart. Toby said nothing, looked at Annie, his eyebrows raised.

'Heartbeat a bit slow, bradycardia,' Annie said. 'But not too slow, so not a tremendously dangerous thing to worry about.'

'Prescribe extra oxygen and organise a cardiorespiratory monitor,' Toby said. 'The nurses will tell us if there's any change.' He grinned, and Annie felt warmth surge through her veins. He went on, 'And I'm going to rub the baby's feet.'

Annie nodded. Rubbing the baby's feet was an ancient remedy, but it often worked.

Then they looked at a baby with cyanosis, a slight blueness of the skin. 'Peripheral, not central,' Toby decided. 'No need to worry, but we'll keep an eye on the condition. Agree?'

'Absolutely.'

These were both small problems, the kind of thing that cropped up every day. But the next case was more serious. Toby went to the nurses' room and came back with Nancy Roberts, a middle-aged midwife with a cheerful disposition. They all looked at baby Helen Carter in her incubator. Helen was very yellow—a sure sign of jaundice.

'Right,' Toby said to Annie, 'for the moment you're in charge. You've looked at the notes and you've examined the baby. Now justify what you're going to do.'

'Me? I came here to watch and help if you needed me!'

'Call it a learning experience. I'm less frightening than a consultant. Aren't I, Nancy?'

'No,' Nancy said with a giggle.

Annie steadied herself and concentrated. When the SHOs were following the consultant on ward rounds, they would often be asked to present a case. It could be a nerve-racking experience, under the watchful eye of the consultant and a handful of your peers. Especially if you were questioned afterwards. She realised that this practice could be useful.

She looked at the notes again and then said, 'The baby presented with jaundice, indicating an inability in the liver to deal with the bilirubin produced. At first phototherapy was tried, and for two days the patient has been exposed continually to a light source, stopping only for feeding and care. However, this treatment has proved ineffective and tests show a rising serum bilirubin level. Now we will replace the baby's blood with fresh, Rhesus negative, ABO compatible blood. This will get rid of excess bilirubin and increase the haemoglobin level.'

'Good,' said Toby. 'Now, I've already passed a catheter into the umbilical vein—where does it go?'

'Through the ductus venosus and into the inferior vena cava.'

'And I've taken a little blood to…?'

'To test for levels of serum bilirubin, haemoglobin and glucose.'

'So now we…?'

'Remove five mils of the baby's blood and replace it immediately with five mils of fresh blood. Then carry on in this way until roughly ninety per cent of the baby's blood has been exchanged.'

'Right. So start.'

Nancy had already fitted the giving set with the donor blood container and the jar to receive the discarded blood. A three-way tap allowed blood to be both fed into the vein and taken from it. Annie opened the tap—and watched as five mils dripped out. Then she reversed the tap and watched as another five mils was introduced into the baby.

For fifteen minutes they watched, saying nothing, until Toby broke the silence. 'OK, everything seems to be fine. The really hard work is now going to be done by Nancy here. She'll stay and watch, she'll record the times and amounts of blood, she'll keep an eye on the electrocardiograph and Helen's temperature.'

'And if anything at all goes wrong, I'll page you,' the midwife said with a smile. 'But things seem to be progressing properly.'

'Good. Now Annie and I can sit and sleep while you do all the work.'

'Always the same,' Nancy said cheerfully. 'See you later, Toby, Annie.'

'You make a point of getting on with the midwives, don't you?' Annie asked as they walked out of the ward. 'You always have the little extra word for them.'

'They do a good job, the experienced ones know more about childbirth than most doctors. I've learned a lot from midwives.'

'Nothing to do with the fact that most of them are female?' The minute she had said it, Annie felt rather guilty. It was wrong to keep reminding Toby of his lady-killer reputation. In effect she had arranged a truce with him so why couldn't she stick to their unspoken agreement? Their affair was over, to be forgotten. From now on they were going to be just friends.

But this time he didn't seem too upset. 'I do like females,' he said evenly, 'but mostly I like midwives because they do a great job and certainly help to make my job easier.'

'I've met more than a few who know far more than me,' Annie agreed. 'But I'm learning. Now, do we need to have a meeting about this new job we're to do together?'

Toby thought a minute. 'It's probably best to wait until John Bennett has told us exactly what he wants. There's no point in making plans until then.'

'True,' Annie said. 'Well, see you, then. I've got these forms to deliver.' She strode off down the corridor. As she walked she was conscious of just the faintest feeling of regret. She would have liked to have continued her conversation with Toby. Just about the new job, of course.

It would have interested her to know that at that moment Toby was feeling exactly the same way. He watched Annie's retreating form and thought how much he was looking forward to working with her. Though he didn't believe for one minute that he could ever be the big brother she had suggested he could be.

As he stood there, lost in thought, his own big brother walked up and stood beside him. Toby guessed that Jack had come to look at the babies he had operated on that morning. In silence, the two of them watched Annie turn a corner and disappear from sight.

'I gather John Bennett has arranged for you to work with Annie at this new clinic,' Jack said.

'So it seems. I'm quite looking forward to it.'

Jack looked serious. 'You're not to mess about with her again Toby. You hurt her before—possibly a lot more than you knew. Perhaps a lot more than you intended.'

'Perhaps so. Don't worry, I'll be the perfect colleague and that's all.'

'Good. If Annie works like she's been doing recently, she'll do well.' Jack slapped his brother on the shoulder and then set off down the corridor.

Toby still had a job to do. He walked back into the ward, smiled at Nancy and said, 'Go and have a break. I'll check things here and watch Helen for a while.'

'Toby, I don't mind staying, honestly. I—'

Toby flapped a hand at her. 'The best medical advice

ever. Given to me by a wise midwife long ago. When you get the chance of a sit-down—take it.'

'OK,' Nancy said reluctantly 'if you really don't need me. Notes here are all up to date. See you in a bit.' She walked down the ward.

Toby checked the notes, checked that there were no leakages in the pipes leading into Helen's umbilicus. All was well. Then he gazed for a moment at the baby they were treating—and his thoughts started to wander again.

He felt—just a bit—that people weren't being altogether fair on him. He had been genuinely sorry to hurt Annie and he now knew he'd hurt her badly. But he had warned her that their affair could only be a casual one. Why was everyone getting at him now? If he'd let things go on much longer, they could have been much worse. He knew what Annie had started to want. There was no way he could have given it to her.

But still…she was over him. Now he was looking forward to working with her. But only as a doctor and a friend, of course.

A week later, Annie was more than happy with her work in the new clinic. It was in a prefabricated unit, about fifty yards from the proper obs and gynae wing. In time a permanent building would be erected there—but for the moment the pre-fab would do very well.

The work was more varied than her work at hospital, she was more her own boss. And what was really pleasant, as promised, she had more time to speak to her patients. They became real people instead of passing figures.

She was also getting on well with Toby. They met often, not only during the lunch-breaks and coffee-breaks they sometimes shared. They had their own tiny doctors' room. And since there wasn't the crowd of other medical staff that there had been in the main hospital, they spent much of their time talking to each other. She was discovering a new side of Toby, a side that she perhaps had not noticed or appreciated during their ill-fated romance. A man who was as dedicated to medicine as his older brother—but a man who went to some lengths to hide his dedication. She was learning from him.

Most of her cases she could deal with reasonably confidently. But if she was in the slightest doubt, she would talk to Toby. Usually, he would reassure her that she had done the right thing. Once or twice they had agreed to refer a case to the registrar. It was as well to be certain.

That morning she was working alone in the postnatal clinic. She should have been working with a midwife but there wasn't one available.

Annie would just have to manage but she was happy with this. So far she had seen five mums and babies—all were in because the district midwife had thought it might be a good idea if they were seen again after what was usually the final examination at four weeks. If all was well at four weeks after a birth, then the work of the obs and gynae department was done.

So far there had been nothing serious discovered. Three of the cases she had signed off, the slight problems had disappeared and in future they would be seen by their own GP. In two cases Annie had issued prescriptions and asked the mums to come back in a fortnight. One had an episiotomy that was not healing; the other had a baby with a chest infection that just would not go away.

Now it was time for the last of her appointments, a Mrs Myers. The district midwife had noted that Stella Myers seemed to be suffering from mild depression. Annie read through the patient's notes, concerned that the depression hadn't yet lifted. After a birth, most women had a few days in which they felt depressed for no particular reason. A few were lucky, their bodies adapted themselves quickly, reverted to the state of health they'd enjoyed before. Other mums had difficulty in coping with the big alteration in their hormones, in the loss—in effect—of thirty per cent of their blood. And there was the sheer impossibility of getting enough sleep. It was an unusual mum who wasn't still tired. Baby blues was common—though usually not serious. And normally it would pass after four weeks or so.

Stella Myers was a well-dressed, attractive woman in her thirties. She was well made-up, and had obviously had a recent visit to an expensive hairdresser's. She had brought Callum, her second baby, and was escorted by her mother. She appeared calm, cool and very much in control.

But the moment she handed the baby to her mother, she promptly burst into tears. 'Doctor, I just can't cope,' Stella wailed. 'I can't sleep. I'm always tired and…and…it all seems as if it will go on for ever. I'm depressed. You've got to give me something.'

'Don't take on so, Stella,' her mother said comfortingly. 'Here, take this tissue then calm down and in a minute you can tell the doctor all about it.'

Annie poured a glass of water and handed it to Stella. 'Sit there and do as your mother says,' she advised with a smile. 'Try to calm yourself. We'll have a chat in a minute, but first I'd like to look at your baby.'

'Thank you, Doctor,' Stella said. She dabbed at her eyes carefully, making sure that her mascara hadn't run.

The examination didn't take long. 'You've got a beautiful, strong, healthy baby here,' Annie said. 'I wish all the babies I see were thriving like Callum.'

Stella shook her head. 'But he cries all the time! Sometimes all through the night!'

Annie resisted the temptation to point out that that's what some babies did. 'It can be very wearing,' she admitted, 'but in time it will pass. Now, if your mother would like to take Callum into the waiting room for a moment, I'd like to examine you.'

In fact, Stella was in apparently equally good shape. Pulse, BP, heart, all were normal—in fact, better than normal. But it was difficult to take accurate readings as she kept up a constant barrage of complaints about how depressed she was.

'Well, I think we've ruled out any physical problem,' Annie said. 'Now let's have a chat about how you feel.'

'I feel helpless. My life's not worth living, and the baby's too much work and it's worst first thing in the morning.'

'I see. Does it get better in the day?'

'A bit,' Stella said reluctantly.

Annie nodded, made a note. 'Now, Stella, I understand that your husband took a fortnight off after the birth...'

There was a set of questions Annie knew to ask. And at the end of them she was in considerable doubt. 'I think,' she said eventually, 'I think that I'd like to consult my colleague, if you don't mind. To get a second opinion.'

'If it's necessary,' Stella sniffed. And Annie went to look for Toby.

Fortunately Toby had finished seeing his patients. He smiled at Annie, and although she was about to consult him on a medical matter, although they were just two colleagues, for a second she felt a jolt low down in her stomach. She shook herself crossly. She was working!

'I've got a patient who claims to be depressed and I'm just not happy,' she told him. 'It's possible that she's...well, she's kidding herself. But it's well over four weeks since the birth of the baby so we have to consider the possibility that she might be heading towards genuine depression.'

Both of them knew that, if untreated, depression could become more and more severe.

Toby looked interested. 'So why aren't you happy?'

'This woman has got everything a mother ought to need. Her husband is supportive and loving, the house is fine, there are apparently no financial worries. She has her family living close by and they're also very support-ive and there's quite a lot of them. In fact, her younger sister's just had a baby, too. The family is delighted with two babies. The mother alternates between the two families.'

'I see. When in the day does she get depressed?'

Annie frowned. 'She said it was bad in the morning but got a bit better as the day progressed.'

'And that tells you?'

'Well, it's unusual. Most genuinely depressed mums start the day well and get worse.'

'True. But still…if there is any chance of depression, you could give her a mild tranquilliser.'

Annie shook her head. 'I don't want to start her on drugs if I can help it.'

'I agree.' Toby thought a moment. 'What was her reaction to the birth of her sister's child?'

'She says she was delighted. And she says that her sister doesn't suffer as she does.'

'Right. Mind if I have a word with her?'

'I'm asking for advice,' Annie told him. 'I'll be happy to learn.'

Toby entered her room and gave the patient and her mother his killer smile. 'Hello, Mrs Myers. I'm Dr Sinclair. I'm sorry to hear you're having troubles, and with such a lovely baby, too.'

With slight irritation Annie noted that Stella seemed to cheer up at the sight of Toby. 'I'm sure you can do something for me, Doctor,' she said.

Toby nodded. 'Dr Arnold here has explained that you're still feeling depressed. But I'm sure we can do something about it. Now, over the past few weeks your body has had enough physical changes, so I don't think we'll be giving you any drugs. Not yet anyway. You owe it to yourself and to your baby to get better nature's way. So I'm going to arrange for you to be visited by a specially trained therapist. She'll be able to counsel you and go through all your worries. She'll help you.'

'But, Doctor, I need something to help me through the day! Perhaps something to calm my nerves and—'

'You don't need anything, Mrs Myers, just your own strength of mind and help from the therapist.'

Annie couldn't help noticing. Toby was still smiling, was still the all helpful doctor. But there was a definite tone in his voice that said that things had gone far enough. And Stella recognised it. 'Of course, Doctor,' she said meekly.

'Then we'll arrange it at once,' Toby said.

'Could it still be genuine depression?' Annie asked ten minutes later. They were sitting in the doctors' room, drinking a welcome cup of coffee.

'If it is, I believe she's brought it on herself,' Toby muttered. 'You can think yourself into being ill, Annie. From what you told me, she appears to have everything she needs, and from what I saw there, she likes to be the centre of attention. And by having a child herself, her sister took that away.'

'So you think it's simple jealousy?'

'It might be jealousy but Mrs Myers would never admit it—even to herself. Especially to herself. She doesn't even realise it. She's got no worries, a loving family, a fine baby. Doesn't she recognise how lucky she is?'

Annie looked at him in surprise. 'Toby, you're getting quite upset about her. What's wrong?'

He shrugged, and she saw the effort he was making to calm down. 'I've seen genuine depression and it's not fun. I've also seen people putting it on like Stella Myers.'

Annie nodded, slightly confused by the uncharacteristic vehemence in Toby's voice, the jumble of emotions in his expression. But before she could say anything, his pager buzzed and the moment was gone.

He looked at the message, reached for the phone in the room, keyed in a number. 'No, nothing at the moment. Certainly will. I'll be there in five minutes.' He hung up and turned to face her, his easygoing smile back in place.

'I'm needed in the delivery suite,' he told her. 'See you later?'

'Later,' she agreed.

When he had gone she wondered just what genuine depression he had seen. Or what was the put-on depression? And why was he concealing it from her? Could he have been depressed himself? The moment she thought of the idea, she laughed. Toby depressed—never! But he had certainly been affected by someone.

'Probably nothing,' the duty registrar told Toby, 'but the midwife was right to call us. Primigravida, her temperature spiked. But it's down to a tolerable level now. I'd like you to keep an eye on things for the next half-hour or so. You've got the time?'

'I've got the time,' Toby said. 'Which room?'

He had been asked to be present at a birth. And he thought that at that moment there was nothing that he would rather do. After what he'd seen today he wanted to witness the happiness, the excitement of the mother. It meant a lot to him.

Unless there was an emergency, the midwife was in charge in the delivery room. If a doctor was there, he was there to assist, not take control. Courteously Toby asked permission to be in the room and then introduced himself to the mum-to-be.

Zoe Gladstone was having her first baby. Her husband was a soldier stationed abroad who couldn't get back home in time for the birth. Her mother was ill. So there was no family member to hold Zoe's hand, to encourage her, to tell her that everything was going well.

The midwife was Angie Quest, a very experienced woman. Toby had worked with her before, knew her to be a miracle of kindness. But she had to attend to the baby as well as Zoe.

Everything appeared to be going well and it was, but he had realised that the tears streaming down Zoe's cheeks were because she was lonely, not so much because of the pain.

So with Angie's permission he stayed for a while, brushed the hair from Zoe's sweat-beaded forehead, had his hand squeezed as the contractions got more frequent. He talked to her, about nothing very much, smiled at her, told her the baby would come soon and she'd know it was all worthwhile. 'You're doing fine,

Zoe,' he said eventually, 'I'll be back when it's all over and you've got a fine baby.'

Zoe's eyes widened. 'You're going? You're not staying to help me?'

He smiled. 'You don't need my help. Angie here is a wonderful midwife—she's brought dozens of babies into the world and knows far more than me.'

'I know but—ow-w! it's nice having you here.'

Toby glanced at Angie who winked and shrugged her shoulders. He thought of what he had to do that afternoon. More paperwork! Well, it could wait. This was hands-on medicine. Formally he asked, 'Would you like me to stay and assist, Angie?'

'I'd be glad of your help. You can take soon.'

'Just have to check in with my partner.' Toby went to an internal phone where he couldn't be overheard and rang Annie's extension. 'If you can manage without me, I'd like to stay down here a bit longer,' he said.

'Problems?'

'Not really. I'm just assisting with a birth.'

'OK. Don't worry, I can cope here.'

They understood each other, Toby thought as he replaced the receiver. They were a good team.

He turned back to the panting mum-to-be. 'When Angie says I can take, that means I get to hold the baby. Don't worry, these are safe hands.' She returned his smile, despite the pain she was in. 'Now, have you thought of names yet? You still don't know if you're having a boy or a girl, do you?'

'What's your name?' Zoe asked.

'I was christened Tobias and I'm called Toby,' he told her. 'And that you don't want. Tobias Gladstone. Never!'

He stayed for the next quarter of an hour, and then it was time. A perfectly straightforward birth, common-place for midwife and doctor. But both of them knew that it was one of the half-dozen most important events in Zoe's life. And they respected that.

Soon it was time to wheel Zoe to the postnatal room. Toby looked down at the pale but smiling new mother, glanced at the little bundle by her side. 'I still think James is a better name than Toby,' he said. 'But you must make your mind up. You know, I really enjoy de-livering babies.'

'That's because you don't have to have one.' Zoe looked at him meaningfully. 'Doctor, it hurts.'

'Quite,' said Toby. 'Quite.'

'You're a bit late,' Annie said as he walked into their doctors' room. 'Been kept busy in Delivery?'

'Just staying a while to observe. One of my patients put me straight about things. It was quite a shock.'

'Put the all-knowing Toby straight! Yes, that must have been a shock to your system. What did she say?'

'I said I enjoyed delivering babies and Zoe Gladstone said that was because I didn't have to have one. She also pointed out that the process hurt.'

'It does? You learn something every day, don't you?' Annie mocked.

'Life is a learning process.' He poured himself a

coffee, came to sit next to her. 'Every day I discover more and more that there are things that I know less and less about.'

'And when I met you first I thought you knew everything! You knew the best place to get a Chinese takeaway, the easiest place to park at hospital, the quickest way to get in and out of town without hiring a taxi.'

'A veritable fount of knowledge.' He looked at the chocolate digestive biscuit she was holding. 'Do you know if there are any chocolate biscuits left in the dispensing machine?'

'Yes,' she said. 'They've all gone. But here.' She handed him what was left of her biscuit.

'I couldn't eat your biscuit!'

'Don't worry. I've had one already. Anyway, I must get off to work.' She stood, made for the door.

'Are you enjoying working here with me?' he called after her. 'Enjoying it as much as I am?'

She stopped, thought a minute. 'Yes, I am,' she said. 'And I quite like working with you. I didn't expect to but we make quite a good medical team don't we?'

'Quite a good medical team indeed.' And she was gone.

He finished her chocolate biscuit, rolled the silver paper into a ball and flicked it expertly into the wastepaper basket.

He'd been working closely with Annie for over a fortnight now and had enjoyed every minute of it. He enjoyed their little medical discussions, enjoyed their joking with each other, in the corridor or in the staff lounge. Their clinic was more intimate than the hospital.

He was friendly with all the staff; there were seldom any strangers in the place. Annie and he were like two members of a family.

He had wondered about working so closely with Annie. But they were doing fine. And she had just said—she quite liked working with him. Did that mean that she quite liked him working aside. Only quite liked? Quite?

A couple more things struck him. He hadn't been out with a girl for—oh, weeks now. And he felt no great need to do so. And when he came into work, if he knew that Annie wasn't going to be there for any reason, he felt disappointed. Not that there was anything between them or going to be anything between them. He knew that couldn't happen. But…she only *quite* liked working with him?

CHAPTER THREE

ANNIE had had a good day, hard but satisfying. In the morning she'd run a clinic. For much of the afternoon she had been at the house of Heather Cross, a girl in the second trimester of her first pregnancy.

There was a problem. Mary Betts, the community nurse, had asked for a second opinion. She wasn't quite sure what was—or might be—wrong. And what made the problem worse was that Heather felt such pain when moving that she said she couldn't come to the hospital for a normal consultation. Although experienced, Mary was new to working in the community, not used to having to work on her own without anyone instantly available to consult. So she had phoned Annie.

'I know that some mothers can feel unspecified pain,' Mary had said, 'and I've had primagravidas who imagine or exaggerate the pain. But so far Heather has been a perfect patient. The baby's wanted, the husband's supportive, Heather's been to all the classes and so on. She's a sensible, level-headed person. And I just don't know where this pain is coming from.'

So Annie had gone round. And she had agreed with all of what Mary had said. Heather appeared to be the perfect mum-to-be. She was prepared, well informed. She was also obviously in great pain when she walked. But after a detailed examination Annie could find no medical reason for it.

It was better to be honest. 'I'm just not sure what's wrong,' Annie confessed. 'I'll take a specimen so we can run a urine test, but I doubt we'll find anything. So I'd like to come back with a colleague to examine you— say, tomorrow?'

Heather was fine with this, but just to be on the safe side Annie stayed a while longer, offering reassurance and checking there were no other concerns or worries, before she finally said goodbye.

'Which colleague are you bringing?' Mary asked as they walked out of Heather's neat little house.'

'Toby Sinclair.'

'Heather will really like him,' Mary said. 'I've worked with him a bit. He's a lovely man, isn't he?'

'A very lovely man,' said Annie. Did Toby have this effect on all the women he worked with? she wondered. Even middle-aged, married women with three children, like Mary? Then she realised she was being unfair. Toby was Toby, everybody's friend.

She had hardly seen him in the morning, not at all in the afternoon. She was quite looking forward to talking about Heather's case with him, trying to decide what was best for her. Probably they would eventually have to bring in a registrar, ask for his diagnosis and learn from him. But it would be nice to have first made a diagnosis of their own.

Toby wasn't in his room. She wrote him a quick note, summarised what she had seen, explained her doubts and asked if he had any free time the next day.

There was a bit of a surprise for her as she walked into the corridor. Calvin was waiting for her, a big smile on his face, a travelling bag in his hand. She was getting on very well with her new flatmate—largely because they rarely met. When they did she found him polite, friendly and considerate, and she felt she'd made a good choice.

Chatting, they went into the doctors' room and Annie started to make the inevitable coffee.

'I'm off down to London for the weekend to see Sarah,' Calvin said. 'I'm not going back to the flat so I brought that magazine I promised you, with the special section on neonatal abnormalities.'

He handed her an American medical magazine. Annie looked at the price, and winced. No wonder the hospital felt it couldn't afford a subscription.

'Thanks a lot, Calvin. I'll get it back to you when I've taken some notes.' Then she thought. 'It's only Thursday. Why the long weekend?'

Calvin's smile grew even broader. 'Celebration time,' he said. 'Big celebration time. My wife is absolutely and properly pregnant. And we're both over the moon.'

'Calvin, I'm so happy for you!' Annie knew that Calvin and Sarah had been trying for a baby for some time. It had just taken a little longer than anticipated. But this was good news.

She was happy for her friend, threw her arms round him and kissed him on the cheek. In sheer delight Calvin hugged her back, lifted her and whirled her round.

The door opened and Toby walked in, closely followed by his twin sister Carly.

'Annie, put Calvin down, he's a married man,' he drawled. 'Carrying on like this in working hours. What will the staff get up to next?'

It was meant to be a joke. But Annie could hear the edge of steel in his voice. Toby was angry. With her?

'It was just my good luck,' said Calvin, blissfully unaware of the undercurrents. 'Hi, Carly.'

'Hi, Calvin,' Carly said. 'How's things? You seem happy.' She had worked with Calvin in Chicago; the two of them were old friends.

Annie realised from Carly's troubled expression that she had detected her brother's ill temper.

'I am happy,' Calvin bubbled on. 'I was just telling Annie here, and now you two can share my good news. My wife is pregnant.'

'Calvin, that's wonderful!' Now Carly came over to kiss Calvin, and Annie saw that Toby looked a little shamefaced.

Calvin hugged Carly as enthusiastically as he had hugged Annie and then said, 'I must go, I've got a train to catch. Hope I can buy some flowers at the station.' And then he was gone.

There was silence for a moment and then Toby mumbled, 'I've got the papers you wanted here.' He opened his locker, took out a folder of notes and handed it to Carly.

'Thanks.' Carly nodded, then went on, 'I'm going to see Jack and Miranda in half an hour—fancy a lift there to visit?'

'Be an idea.'

'I'll come back for you.' Carly left.

Annie said nothing. Toby poured himself a coffee and offered Annie one.

'Thank you, no.' The silence continued.

Toby tried again. 'Good news for Calvin, isn't it? He's got what he's been wanting. The man's so pleased that he's positively radiant.'

'Isn't he just?' Now it was Annie's turn to have steel in her voice. She went on, 'You know, Toby, when you came in and found Calvin hugging me, I could have sworn that you were upset. Angry even.'

Toby was instantly on the defensive. 'Me? Upset? What have I got to be upset about? Seeing you and Calvin just took me by surprise for a moment. Anyway, it's nothing.'

'You're right, it was nothing. I'm only glad that Calvin didn't notice how you felt, but at the moment he's so happy the entire world is his friend. But Carly certainly noticed.'

'There was nothing to notice.' Toby's voice was distinctly uneasy.

Annie hadn't been too sure how she felt. She knew she felt something—but what was it? And now she was certain. It was pure, scorching anger. For quite a while now she had been getting on quite well with Toby. She liked his company, enjoyed working with him. But suddenly, with just one look and one careless expression, he had brought out feelings that she thought she'd buried.

'What right had you to feel angry at my being with someone?' she snarled.

This time he didn't bother to deny the accusation. 'No right,' he admitted.

'No right at all. You know, Toby, I've been easy on you. You dumped me. I suppose that was your right. And I did what you knew I'd do. I accepted it and made as little fuss as possible. I know that you told me that our affair was only for fun, was only going to be something casual, but your body said more than your mouth did. When we were together I felt that we were making love—not having casual sex. And that typical male excuse—*Don't fall for me, I'm not worth it.* Well, I did fall for you, Toby, and you should have known I would, and it hurt.'

Silent he stared at her, his eyes wide with shock.

Then, in a perfectly normal voice she said, 'Sorry about that. It was most unprofessional. It won't happen again. Please, forget it.'

''I…I'm sorry I upset you,' he muttered eventually. 'I didn't really know… Is there anything I can do?'

'Pour me that coffee, please. I'm going to freshen up.'

She left. After washing her face in cold water and putting on fresh make-up, Annie went back to the doctors' room. There was no Toby, just a cup of newly made coffee, a saucer on top of it. And a little handwritten note—*Sorry, got a call to make.*

Perfectly calmly, Annie sat and drank the coffee.

* * *

Toby didn't have a call to make, he just needed to be alone. He sat at his desk in his room, feeling bewildered.

He thought he had been, well, reasonable with Annie. She was right in one respect—he had ended their affair because he knew she was getting far too fond of him. And perhaps he was getting too fond of… No. Forget that.

For a moment he wondered if he should tell the real, honest truth about why they'd had to part. But the thought frightened him. No way could he do that. No one in this hospital knew—not even his older brother or twin sister.

He didn't want comfort; he knew there could be none. So there was no point in telling her. And people would only try to help. He didn't want help; he'd learned to cope with things on his own. In his own way.

He was still thinking when Carly came in to take him to visit Miranda and Jack. 'Want to say goodnight to Annie?' Carly asked. 'I saw her in one of the treatment rooms.'

He tried to be his normal urbane self. 'No need really. I've said it once already.'

'Right.' Carly led him to her car, said nothing until they were safely out of the hospital grounds. Then, 'So what exactly are your feelings for Annie now?' Carly asked.

He jerked. They were twins, but quite different in character. How come she could suddenly read his mind? 'What do you mean?' he asked. 'I haven't got any feelings for Annie. Well, I like her and I like working with her. She's a good doctor.'

'There's more to it than that. I saw your anger when you saw her with Calvin.'

'It was nothing, perhaps surprise,' said Toby. 'I was just tired.'

But he was shocked. Was he so transparent? He was supposed to be the one who could conceal his feelings.

'I remember the short time you were together with Annie,' Carly went on. 'You seemed very happy together. It didn't last long but you seemed to be getting closer to her than anyone for a while. You looked to be the ideal couple.'

'Carly! Can you stop talking about this? You're imagining things. It's stupid and it's pointless.'

'My, my. What's upsetting my twin brother? Where's the easygoing chap that everyone knows?'

'Just change the subject,' he said tersely.

There was a pause. 'I'll change the subject. Remember the year when you were a houseman at St Mark's Hospital in London? Your first job after you graduated?'

Now this was getting serious. He tried to calm himself, make sure that his voice was careless. Difficult when she was bringing up memories he had tried to keep buried for so long. 'Sure I remember. I worked harder then than I've ever worked in my life.'

'Quite so. Now, I know you aren't the greatest of correspondents, but I hardly had a letter from you for two entire years.'

'I told you, I was working too hard.' He could hear his voice shaking and willed himself to stay cool.

'Weren't we all? But I still wondered—'

'Carly, drop it.'

There was silence in the car again for a while, but then Carly persisted. 'Toby, what happened?'

'Nothing happened.'

'You'd better tell someone some time,' she told him gently. 'You might think you can keep it hidden, but it's eating you up inside.'

Now they had, in effect, their own clinic, Annie and Toby were left to organise their own timetables. They weren't constantly at the beck and call of the registrars and the consultant. It was promotion of a sort and they both liked it.

Next morning they both had appointments lists. Annie didn't see Toby before she started work, and wondered how he might react after her outburst yesterday. She had thought about it, asked herself if she should feel guilty about what she had said. Then she had decided that there was no need to feel guilty. It was right that he should know exactly what her emotions had been. She felt better for telling him. She felt that a corner had been turned in their relationship. Now they could progress. And she wanted to progress.

She met him first in the corridor at the midmorning break. Even though his smile was perhaps a bit cautious, he gave her his usual cordial greeting.

'Got your note about Heather Cross,' he said when she had smiled back. 'I can easily make time this afternoon. Shall we go to see her together?'

'That'd be great.' She decided to be completely

honest. 'I'm just lost. But I'd like it if we could decide what's wrong ourselves, instead of referring it upstairs.'

'Me, too. Say, two o'clock, go in my car?'

'Two o'clock suits me fine.' Good. Annie felt better. Yesterday's scene had been...well, she knew it wouldn't be forgotten, but for the moment it would not be referred to. Probably the best thing. Then she remembered that Toby had been going to see Jack and Miranda. She hadn't heard from her friend for a while. 'How's the happily engaged couple?' she asked.

'Happily planning their wedding. I stayed with them for a while then we all went over to see my mother.'

'How is she?'

Annie knew that Carly, Toby and Jack were devoted to their mother. She was dying of brain-stem cancer. When they'd found out about it, Carly and Toby had arranged their training so they could be near her.

Perhaps other people wouldn't have noticed. But Annie had spent a lot of time looking at Toby's face, often when he had not been aware of it. And she saw the wince of pain as he mumbled, 'Well, she's not too bad. She comes and goes, you know.'

In a gentle voice she said, 'Toby, I know you, I know all your family. I'm concerned. Give me an honest answer. How is your mother?'

He sighed. 'She's slipping away. She knows it, we all know it. She's accepted it. I don't think that we have.' She watched as the sadness was quickly masked by his usual cheerful expression. 'Now, I haven't had coffee for at least an hour and I—'

She interrupted him. 'You know, you don't have to move into the cheerful Toby, always happy act. You are entitled to feelings and you're entitled to show them.'

For a moment she thought she'd reached him. 'It's the way I cope,' he said simply. 'So, two o'clock, my car, we'll go and see Heather Cross. Will you phone the midwife, see if it's all right with her?'

'No problem.'

And there was no problem. 'It'll be good to see Toby again,' Mary said. 'Is he as lovely as ever?'

'Will he ever change?' asked Annie with a wry smile.

Annie had to admit that Toby was as lovely as ever. Mary let them into Heather's house and Toby said, 'I've not seen you for a couple of months, Mary. How's Ben getting on in his new school? I remember you were a bit doubtful about it.'

Mary smiled happily. 'Ben's doing fine, I was silly to worry. I'll tell him you were asking. Now, Heather's looking forward to seeing you both. I think she gets a bit bored, just lying here all day. Usually she's one of the world's workers.'

Mary led them to the living room. As the day before, Heather was lying on the couch, She sat up and turned as they walked in, then she saw Toby and turned even faster. And then she grimaced with pain.

Toby walked forward, put an arm round her shoulders and eased her backwards. 'Just take it easy, Mrs Cross. I'm Dr Sinclair. We've come here to have a quick look at you, see if we can do anything about this pain. I know that so far you've had the best of care from Mary here but let's see if we can find out exactly what's wrong.'

He was good, Annie thought as she watched a much calmer Heather lie back on her couch, asking Toby to call her by her first name. A smiling Toby could make anyone relax. She remembered how he'd used the same technique on her...but, no, it wasn't a technique. It was just Toby himself.

There was a few minutes' chat. Toby then examined Heather and after a while agreed with Mary and Annie that mother and baby seemed to be doing fine and he couldn't find anything organically wrong.

'We can't send you for a scan or an X-ray,' he told Heather, 'as they might harm the baby. So tell me more about this pain.'

'It started about week twenty-five,' Heather recalled. 'Everything had been fine until then. It happens when I'm walking usually, this sudden biting pain, down here, the baby bit. And inside my thighs and sometimes over the lower bit of my back. It's got so bad that I have to sleep down here, I just can't get upstairs. I'm lying here and I don't want to. My husband is so good. He comes home and he does everything for me.'

Tears formed in Heather's eyes. 'I've asked Mary here and she says it's all right so long as I'm comfortable with it. But I can't let my husband make love to me. I want to but I just can't get my legs apart.'

Suddenly, Toby looked alert. 'Tell me exactly what it feels like when you walk.'

'It feels as if there's bones grinding. And sometimes there's a sort of…of…'

'Clicking?'

'How did you know that?' Heather asked.

Toby nodded. 'Diastasis symphysis pubis,' he said. 'Don't get alarmed! The name is the worst thing about it. You and the baby are both safe. There's going to be no long-term problems.'

He pointed to Heather's hips. 'Your two hip bones nearly meet here. They're joined together at the front by strong cartilage, called the symphysis pubis. When you are pregnant the cartilage relaxes a bit—about two or three millimeters—so the baby's head can get through more easily. But sometimes it relaxes too much—and all the other joints get strained. It's a mechanical thing.'

'So what do I do?'

He smiled reassuringly. 'First of all, don't worry. But you have to take things easy. If you walk upstairs, take one step at a time. We'll give you painkillers and Mary here will fit you with a pelvic support garment. Even crutches might help. I'll send you a few very easy exercises to do.'

'And having the baby will be all right?' Heather was still anxious, although it was obvious that Toby's confident manner had calmed her.

'Now we know what's wrong, we can take precautions. You have to find the most comfortable way of giving birth. For example, you might try it on all fours. You're not to try to get your legs too far apart—Mary will measure you to find out what is comfortable.'

'And will I be all right afterwards?'

'You'll have to take things easy for six months or so. No straining or heavy lifting. But then you should be back to normal.'

Heather smiled, relief clearly visible in her face. 'That's wonderful. I feel so much better. Now I know there's a cause and that there's no long-term danger, I can put up with it.'

'We'll make you more comfortable,' Toby promised. 'And if Mary doesn't mind, Annie and I would like to drop in to see you now and again.'

'That would be lovely. Now, can I stagger to the kitchen and make you a cup of tea?'

'We'll do it ourselves,' said Toby.

'I learned something there,' Annie said as they drove off in Toby's car. 'Thanks for the lesson, Toby.'

'I like working with mothers and children,' Toby said. 'I like it when all is going well or I can give good news.'

To Annie's surprise she saw that his face was bleak rather than elated. 'I like it, too,' she said. 'And since you've just given someone good news, why are you looking so gloomy?'

He didn't answer for a while. Then he turned off the main road, turned again and stopped. Annie blinked. They were in a cul-de-sac, a quiet shaded spot near the top of a tiny hill, and in front of them was a vista of trees. It struck her as the kind of place that lovers might visit in the evening.

To her surprise he reached over, took one of her

hands and held it in both of his. She was so shocked that she didn't try to pull it away. What was he doing?

'I want to say something about what you said to me yesterday,' he said. 'Although I suspect you're not very keen to talk about it.'

'I meant what I said and now I realise that I had to say it,' said Annie slowly. 'But now it's over and I'm happy to forget it. After all, we do work well together. And what are you doing, holding my hand?'

Toby didn't answer for a moment, just looked puzzled, as if he didn't actually know the answer to her question. Gently, he squeezed her hand and she had to admit to herself that she liked it. But then she pulled it away.

'We're friends,' he muttered. 'Can't friends hold hands?'

'Not if they used to be lovers. Anyway, you have lots of female friends to hold your hand—lots of lovers, in fact. You apparently need that rich variety.'

'I've not been out with anyone since I left you, Annie.'

This surprised her. 'Not one? Why not?'

He didn't seem to know what to reply. Then, 'I just can't get interested.'

'What, you? The great lover? Can't get interested?'

She watched him struggle for a while. For the first time ever she found him at a loss for words. Eventually he said, 'I think I might have made a big mistake when I finished with you,' he confessed. 'I think that you and me might have had…something going.'

Might have had something going? Toby Sinclair, that is the most feeble declaration of love I've ever heard.' She thought a moment, wondered if she was going to get angry. But she knew that would do her no good and now she was curious. '"You and me might have had something going,"' she quoted. 'I thought we had a lot of something going. But you stopped it. Why Toby?

She unclipped her safety belt, leaned across so their faces were close together. 'I told you yesterday but you seem to have forgotten already. Toby, you hurt me and it's not going to happen again. I still think you're attractive—I'm one of many, aren't I? Don't worry, I'm going to fight it.'

She slammed back in her seat, stared at the wooded horizon. 'It hurt because it seemed pointless. I knew you felt what we had, we were good for each other. Now even you talk about us having something going. Well, what went wrong?'

He thought a moment and then said, in an almost abstracted way. 'Can you believe I was thinking of you? That I was doing what I thought best for you?'

'You have a funny way of showing it. But you could try to convince me.'

Once again he reached over for her hand, and once again she let him take it. He lifted it to his lips, kissed it gently. Then he sighed. He put her hand back in her lap, reached to turn on the car engine. What discussion there was to be was over, Annie realised.

'You just can't believe me when I say that I was trying to be kind?' he asked as they backed out of the little cul-de-sac.

'It's a bit hard to,' she told him.

* * *

That evening Miranda called round. She had left a few things stored in the flat and wanted to pick them up. As Calvin was in London, the two women settled down to drink red wine and gossip. There was a wedding to be planned!

Of course, however, the conversation soon turned to Toby. 'How are you getting on with Toby?' Miranda asked.

Annie sighed. 'Sort of all right. But, Miranda, there's something I don't know about him. He's… What is he really like?'

Miranda frowned. 'I thought things were going well. I was concerned because I know, even though you tried to hide it from me, that you were hit pretty hard when you parted.'

'Things are going well! Quite well, anyway. It's just that sometimes…I feel that underneath that happy big smiling exterior there's another Toby that I don't know. Perhaps a sad Toby. I feel I'm missing something.'

'I could ask Jack,' Miranda offered, and picked up the phone.

'No, don't do that! I don't want to pry and I don't want to upset the family.'

'I'm family now,' Miranda pointed out. 'Well, nearly family. And so I'm entitled to pry. In fact, I know that Jack worries about Toby—far more than he ever does over Carly. He says he's not the lad he remembers—but Carly is just the same.'

She tapped in a number. 'Hi, Jack. It's me. Look, family secrets. I'm talking to Annie. You know she's working with Toby? Well, they're getting on well enough, but Annie feels she's missing something. Something that's making him not very happy. Any ideas?'

Annie watched as Miranda listened for quite a while, then said goodbye to Jack and switched off her phone.

'First of all—don't need to tell you but this is for your ears only.'

'Of course.'

'Well, there's something interesting. Jack says that Toby and Carly are twins but are very different. Carly is usually open with her feelings, but Toby has always been much less so. That happy exterior is him all right—but it's also a show. And it's got worse—or better, I don't know. He used to be much more serious, but a couple of years ago things changed. There were few visits from him, few letters, few phone calls. After that, Toby the clown.'

'So what happened?'

'No one knows. Something seems to have given him a shock. It might be that he knew his mother was getting ill—but Jack doesn't think that it's that. Possibly he's just grown that way—people do change, you know.' Miranda shrugged. 'I'd like to help him. He helped me and Jack get together.' She stood, reached over to hug her friend. 'But now I'd better go. Been good seeing you. And, whatever you do, don't get hurt again.'

Annie's tone was firmer than she actually felt. 'I won't. There's absolutely no chance of that.'

There was still half a bottle of red wine left. Annie poured herself another glass, kicked off her shoes and stretched her legs along the couch. Interesting, what

Miranda had said. Toby had changed a couple of years ago. Really changed. His family had seen little of him.

Of course, there could be all sorts of reasons. Annie remembered the hectic time of her own exams when social life, friends, family had all seemed to take second place to the all-important work. And she knew Toby was a worker. But why had he changed? She wondered if she could find out.

She took a mouthful of red wine then closed her eyes and thought about him. Tall, athletic Toby, always smiling, always—nearly always—kind. Easy to talk to, far too easy to fall in love with, as she'd found to her cost.

And he was such a good doctor. She thought of their work in the clinic together, how he put people at ease, how astute he could be when diagnosing. And he was inexhaustibly patient.

Why was her glass empty? She poured herself more wine.

She remembered sitting on this very couch with him—yes, and drinking red wine—how they had watched a DVD together. They had both agreed at the end that it was a lovely story but that the characters could have hurried things along a little. 'They both know what's going to happen,' Toby had pointed out, 'and they both want it to happen. So why hang about?'

'Putting things off a bit prolongs the pleasure,' she had said primly. 'It's like unwrapping a present. You do it slowly.'

It had been an idle, self-indulgent evening. They had both had a hard-working week, had seen little of each other. All they'd wanted had been to be together, to do nothing very much. He had brought round a couple of bottles of wine; she had ordered an Indian takeaway. And after eating they'd watched the film.

Annie remembered that night with a special clarity. Suddenly she'd been aware that she hadn't felt tired any more. She had been half sitting half lying on Toby's lap. His arms had been round her, supporting her, when he'd wanted to, he'd eased her to him and kissed her. So far, just gentle, reflective kisses. But then had come a kiss of a different kind. And she had looked up into his smoky eyes and known that the kiss had been almost a question, and that the answer had to be yes. Her arms had tightened round him. She had pressed her body against his, an unspoken answer to an unspoken question.

And then they went to bed. And, no, they didn't have sex; they made love. Although nothing was said, she knew it, felt it. She knew that he loved her, too.

Four weeks later he finished with her and the happiest weeks of her life turned into the most miserable.

Annie reached for the bottle. Her glass was empty. Then she blinked. The bottle was empty, too. She had finished it. So much for wandering down memory lane. Thinking about Toby had caused her to...

Then it came crashing down on her, a realisation that was shocking in its certainty. How could this have happened? For the last few weeks she had been congratulating herself that she had finally got over the pain of parting from Toby. They had started a new relationship, they had become friends, they were working well together.

All that had been a lie. Tears ran down her cheeks as she tried to cope with what she now knew. She loved Toby as much as she had ever done.

CHAPTER FOUR

IT WAS her first conscious thought when Annie woke next morning. She loved Toby. She'd never stopped loving him. And now the uncertainty, the anxiety she had felt the night before was ebbing. She loved Toby. She had been fooling herself when she'd thought she could work with him and pretend that there was nothing between them. There was something there. The question was, what did she do about it?

She climbed out of bed, and as she set about preparing breakfast she cool-headedly considered her options. Perhaps, painful though it would be at first, she should get as far from him as possible. She could leave the clinic, ask to be moved back to ordinary duties. There were plenty of other SHOs who would like her place. At the end of her six months rotation, in another couple of months, she could even apply to another hospital. It wouldn't be too long and she wouldn't have to see much of him.

Then she decided that no way was she going to run. She could bear being with him, she *would* bear being with him. Pictures of him flashed across her mind. Toby smiling at her, Toby leaning over a cot and tickling a baby's face, Toby laughing among friends. Irresistible, commitment-shy, heartbreaker Toby. How could someone she felt so much for cause her so much misery?

Then the thought of what he had said to her yesterday flashed across her mind. What was it…that he had made a mistake in finishing with her? That he thought that they might have had something going, and there had been a definite reason for their parting? Well, if that was true, she was entitled to know what it was and she intended to find out.

Then she felt a touch of shame. She had a secret of her own that perhaps Toby was entitled to know. Too bad. She would start her campaign at once. Whatever Toby was keeping from her, she was going to know. She couldn't just suffer.

It was a typical morning at the clinic. They both had patients to see, work they both enjoyed. Both were hurrying as they met by accident in the corridor, just having time for a smile and a quick word. When she saw him coming towards her, her heart beat just a little more quickly than it should. And she realised that that instant reaction had never gone away. Every time she saw him she felt him, deep within her. She used to think it was nerves, now she knew it was more than that. It was just his presence.

The usual beaming smile, but no time for a long chat. Just a typical Toby remark. 'I've been administrating already,' he proclaimed loftily, 'making your life and mine much easier. The machine ran out of chocolate biscuits. I've contacted management and they've assured me that the machine will be resupplied at once.'

She managed a response. Shaking her head, she said, 'The place would fall to bits without you, Toby.' Then she hurried to her treatment room.

It was hard but she forced herself to work. She was not entitled to personal feelings while her patients had anxieties, problems of their own. She was a doctor!

As usual, they met in the midmorning break. Usually there were just the two of them in the doctors' room, she was relying on this. She arrived a little early, made the coffee and even bought him the requisite chocolate biscuit. She had decided there were things she needed to know and she wanted to make sure that he knew what she wanted. Expecting him, she was ready to start her inquisition. But there was still that feeling, that pang of desire, when he walked into the room.

His coffee was poured, his biscuit ready. 'Must be my birthday,' he said, biting into the chocolate. 'Anything interesting in this morning?'

Now to start. 'Nothing as interesting as yesterday,' she told him. 'I think you're getting away with things, Toby. Yesterday, when we were stopped in the car, you told me that you thought you'd been kind to me. I didn't quite agree. Well, don't worry, I'm not going to go over all that again. As lovers we're finished.'

She lifted her coffee-cup to her lips, hiding her face as she wondered how she could lie so easily. It wasn't easy. She went on, 'But I am interested in why you being kind should result in so much misery for me. I think I'm entitled to know.'

For a moment she thought she'd got to him. He looked sad, started to speak several times and then stopped. But then his face looked blank and Annie, who now understood all his expressions, knew that he was not going to tell her anything. Or so he thought. He said, 'Annie, we're working well together now. I told you I was really sorry for what I did. Isn't it better that we just forget things and—'

There was a knock on the door and Eva, their receptionist, looked in and said, 'Toby, there's a woman at the desk, demanding to talk to you. Demanding to talk to you now.'

'Ask her to have a seat and tell her I'll be out in ten minutes.'

The receptionist shook her head. 'I've tried that but she gets hysterical. She says if you don't talk to her she'll scream the place down. I just don't know what's wrong with her. Quite an old lady, too, and she does look a bit ill.'

Toby sighed. 'I'll come and see what I can do,' he said.

Annie was annoyed. This was typical. Just when she wanted to carry on an argument, some woman came and interrupted her. And when Toby didn't come straight back she grew more annoyed still.

Toby felt troubled as he walked along the corridor behind Eva. He'd thought things between him and Annie had been working out quite well. He had hated hurting her and had hoped that they had started a new friendly relationship with the past left firmly behind. But that wasn't good enough for her. She needed an explanation. Toby could sympathise—in her position he'd feel the same way. Should he tell her? For a moment he was tempted. Then he grimaced. Not a good idea. He knew Annie. She'd be angry at first. But then she'd want to help. And he didn't need help. Now, who was this woman so determined to speak to him?

He walked into the reception area.

The woman was tall, aged about sixty, quite well dressed. Toby thought there was something in her face that he recognised. But he wasn't sure what. In her face he could see signs of fear, of strain. He guessed recent heart trouble. But what was she doing in an obs and gynae clinic?

'Dr Sinclair? This won't take long. Shall we talk outside a moment?'

The woman didn't smile or hold out her hand. She was calm now, her glance indicating that she did not care to have their conversation overheard by the obviously curious Eva.

Toby was curious himself now. He followed the woman to a dark-coloured classic sports car. She turned and said, 'We haven't met before. My name is Ursula de Sangrail. I am—or was—your mother-in-law.'

Toby gazed at her, his thoughts spinning wildly before he was able to speak. 'What can I do for you, Mrs de Sangrail?' he managed.

'You heard from our solicitors of the tragic death of my daughter—your ex-wife?'

'I did. A letter with exactly five lines in it.' Toby struggled a bit and then said, 'I'm sorry for your loss.'

'Quite so. But Gail's death leaves us with a problem. I have been having problems myself—I have angina and, of course, this made things much worse. My doctors advise me that I must avoid all stress. I'm thinking of going on a cruise—one suitable to people in my state.'

Toby felt a sense of unreality growing inside him. 'A cruise might be a good idea,' he said. 'Why does it concern me?'

'This is what concerns you.' The woman moved to one side, unlocked the car door. Toby peered in. The back and front seats were piled with boxes, cases, assorted other gear. In the middle of the back seat there was a child's car seat. And in that seat was a child.

'Your son, Charlie,' the woman said.

'What?' Toby grasped the car door for support and stared at the woman.

'This is your son, Charlie. To be exact, Charles Adam Sinclair. Gail gave him your name to save herself trouble.'

'But…that's impossible! Gail wasn't even pregnant and we always—'

'Gail certainly was pregnant. She might not have told you, but she gave birth five months after you divorced.' Mrs de Sangrail waved her hand at a package in the car. 'I was anticipating this reaction from you. There are all sorts of medical details in there, including the baby's DNA. Have it checked against your own DNA. He's certainly your son.'

'So Gail had to check, did she?' Toby asked bitterly. 'I might have guessed.'

For a moment he was silent, looked around at the sky, the distant buildings of the hospital, watched a couple of nurses hurrying along a path. Not ten minutes ago his life had been calm, serene; he had been happy. And now…

'So what are your plans for my…my son?' he said eventually, his words sounding fuzzy and indistinct in his ears.

'I'm leaving him here with you. You are his father. I'm not well enough to look after him.' Ursula stared at him fiercely. 'You must accept your responsibilities. If you don't—or won't—I'll have no choice but to arrange for him to be taken into care.'

Toby leaned into the car, peered at the small sleeping face. His son?

'Help me get everything out of the car,' Mrs de Sangrail said. Then, for the first time since she'd come charging into his life, she looked sad, uncertain, her eyes pleading with Toby to understand, despite everything that had happened. 'I'm too old to be a mother again. Charlie needs you, Dr Sinclair. His father.'

It was fifteen minutes before Toby returned. He had on that blank, bland expression that Annie knew so well— and disliked so much. And by this time she was enraged. Sarcastically, she said, 'It must be tough, being you. I'm surprised you have time to get any work done, the number of disturbed women hanging round you. Don't you ever get tired of it all?'

His face went white. 'If you knew what you were talking about, you might not be so ready to pass judgement. Now I'm taking the rest of the day off.' He turned and slammed out of the door.

Annie looked after him, open-mouthed. Something must have really upset him. Had she upset him? Or this other woman…?

Annie shrugged. Time might tell what was wrong. But in the meantime she had just one patient left. But even as she carefully listened to her patient's troubles, she wondered. What had happened?

At the end of the day, Annie was finishing her paperwork when the phone rang.

'Annie, it's Toby. Look, I'm so sorry I shouted at you. I know what you said was a joke, and I suppose a joke I deserve. But…' His voice trailed away.

This wasn't the man she knew. 'Toby, is something wrong?' Now she was concerned.

'You could say that. Annie, could you come round and see me after work?'

This was unusual. 'I suppose I could. Why?'

'Something's happened and I don't know what to do. Could you just come over?'

He sounded desperate, Annie thought. She'd never heard him sound like this before. For a moment she wondered if he was playing some kind of complicated smart trick on her, but that just wasn't Toby. In some ways he was very honest. But still… 'Come to your flat? Just for a talk?'

His laugh was painful. 'I know what you're thinking

but it's not that at all. It has to be my flat. You'll see why when you get there.'

By now she was intrigued. 'I could be there about seven,' she said. 'Will that do?'

'I guess that would be fine. Thanks, Annie. I really appreciate this' And he hung up.

Annie found it hard to concentrate. What could Toby possibly want with her? What was so important? Was it to talk about their relationship? Somehow she didn't think so. But she'd go and offer him what advice he needed. And after that it would be her turn for some answers.

His flat door was ajar. So she rang the bell, then stepped into the tiny hall and shouted his name. He shouted back. 'Come in, Annie, and shut the door.' Not like Toby. Normally he would have come out to greet her—he was always courteous that way.

And she heard something else. A wailing sound, almost like a baby. Odd. Maybe it came from a neighbour's flat

She had been to his place before. In fact, she had made love with him there. And when she entered the hall she felt a great surge of memory, of the joy they had brought each other there. Pity it had ended.

She walked into the living room.

The flat was smaller than hers. His attitude to home was like his attitude to clothes. He liked to be neat, tidy, but a bit exciting. She would never have painted her living-room walls red, but it certainly worked for Toby. She always took pleasure in glancing at the pictures on his wall, too. Good reproductions of Impressionists and…

What was this? Eyes, mouth, opened in incredulity. The normally neat room was filled with cases, boxes, most opened and their contents spilling out. And there was Toby. His hair was more tousled than ever, his face harassed, a towel wrapped round his waist. He was standing behind the living-room table. To one side of the table was a pile of towels, a pile of clothes, a bowl of water. In the middle of the table was a changing mat, and on the mat was a naked baby. Toby was holding the baby's feet in one hand, dabbing ineffectually at the baby's bottom with a flannel in the other hand. The baby started to cry.

'This is a lot harder than it looks,' Toby said, managing a smile. 'Some people make it seem so easy.'

Annie just stared, so he continued.

'Meet Charles Adam Sinclair. My son.'

Annie looked at him, appalled. 'You didn't tell me you had a child!'

'I didn't know myself until an hour ago.' Toby turned, and his elbow knocked the pile of clothes into the bowl of water. 'So it's been quite a shock for me, too. And as you can see, Charlie's not very happy with me at the moment,' he said, as the baby's wails increased.

Annie was speechless. She didn't know whether to be angry, surprised, amused or horrified. A thousand emotions fought within her. Toby had a baby! But he was against commitment, against having babies— having them himself, that was. If he had a baby then he must have had—there must have been a woman involved. Well, obviously. Why hadn't he told her? She wanted a baby herself in time and now…

It was all too much; she couldn't cope. Much easier to take refuge in simple actions. 'If you're trying to bathe that baby, you're doing it all wrong,' she said. 'Shall I show you?'

'Thanks, Annie. It's something I've got to learn.' He handed the baby over to her and she cradled Charlie to her, loving how he felt in her arms.

She'd enjoyed helping to look after her cousin's two young children when they had been babies, washing, dressing, feeding and playing with them. Those skills would certainly come in useful now.

She rocked the little scrap of humanity given to her. There was that baby smell, those blue unquestioning eyes, that little mouth that opened, yawned and shut again. It was all too much, there were too many feelings. What did she feel for Toby now? It was hard to tell. There was great sympathy but also great anger. She felt that he had managed to make a mess of his life—and in doing so had managed to make a mess of hers, too

Pushing her emotions aside, she washed the now quiet baby, put on his nappy and dressed him in the clothes that Toby handed her, turning chaos into peaceful orderliness. 'Is he due a feed?'

'I think so. There's a bottle somewhere and packets of stuff and some pots of goo as well.'

She handed the baby to him, Charlie looking so small and safe in his arms. 'Here, nurse your son. Walk up and down with him. You know they like movement. Lean his head over your shoulder.'

Toby did as he was told, watching while Annie mixed

a feed, warmed a pot of beef and rice. Then she showed Toby how to sit and hold the baby, how to feed him, how to keep a towel over his shoulder. He sat quite contentedly, the baby in his lap. And Annie cleared away the table, took a while to survey what else needed to be done, checked over the contents of the various boxes. Practically everything needed for a baby was there, and all of good quality. Toby appeared to have acquired a baby who apparently needed nothing. Except a loving family.

She came to sit opposite him. Now he knew what he was doing he appeared quite contented. In fact, there was a smile, half surprised, half curious.

She had to examine her own emotions again. There was a sense of anger and betrayal. He had kept things from her that she ought to have known. He had claimed that he didn't want commitment—that was why he had got rid of her. And yet he had been committed enough with someone to have a baby. And she'd wanted a baby! He just hadn't been fair.

'You said you wanted my advice,' she said. 'I'm not sure I'm the right person to give it. For a start, I don't feel very detached. But let's start at the beginning. Why didn't you tell me you had a child?'

'Like I said, I didn't know,' he said simply, gazing down at his son's tiny features. 'The first knowledge I had of it was an hour and a half ago.'

'What?'

'I'll be brief and then you can ask questions. Maybe I should start from the beginning. Two years ago, I got married.'

Annie felt the ice form around her heart as she heard this. At first she could hardly comprehend what he had said. Toby? Married? But they had… It was a while before she could speak. 'Well, that's nice to know,' she said, her voice strangely calm. 'Don't you think you might have mentioned being married before? Say, before you took me to bed?'

He shook his head. 'I wasn't married when I took you to bed. By that time I was divorced.'

Annie was still shocked by what she had heard. 'Married and divorced inside two years? Somebody certainly made a mistake.'

'I made a mistake. We made a mistake. I thought I was in love, I really did.' Distracted, he pushed his free hand through his unruly hair. It was a familiar gesture and as he made it her heart lurched again, aching for him. Then she was angry at herself. How could she feel for him when he was confessing this?

'The baby, Toby?'

'Our marriage lasted six months. Then we divorced and parted, vowing never to meet again. That was about eighteen months ago, just before I came here to start as an SHO. And we hated each other. No problems about settlements or upkeep, she came from a very rich family. Annie, I had no idea she was pregnant.'

'She didn't tell you she was pregnant? Toby, how could you not know?'

'She would have only been about three months pregnant when we parted. And she kept it from me. She kept a lot of things from me.'

Annie was having difficulty taking all this in. 'And why the baby now?'

'Gail—that was her name—died a short while ago in an accident. She lived with her mother, who has decided that she can't cope with the baby. So she brought him to me.'

'And you didn't even know Charlie existed?'

'No.'

'So how do you feel now?'

He sighed. 'Annie, for the first time in my life I feel this is something I don't know how to cope with.'

'You're not thinking of having the baby taken into care?'

He looked up sharply. 'Never. I face up to my responsibilities.'

Annie looked at the baby. 'He's beautiful,' she said softly. 'Wipe his face with one of those wet wipes then put him over your shoulder and wind him.'

As Toby did as she told him, Annie considered his options. It was better for her to be cool, logical. Planning something took her mind off her own problems. But she knew there'd have to be a reckoning between her and Toby later. When his present precarious situation was easier.

'Can you get any time off work?' she asked.

'Already have done, starting today. John Bennett's given me a week. I said family problems—I didn't say exactly what.'

'Probably wise. I suppose the question now is, what do you want of me?' she said flatly.

He nodded. 'I want to do the best for Charlie, but I

need to make sure I'm looking after him properly,' he said. 'And…of course, you have every right to say no, but I'd really appreciate your support, Annie. Just until things are settled and I'm confident enough to care for him on my own.'

Her thoughts racing, she didn't immediately answer, and Toby continued. 'If you walked out of here right now, I'd understand. It would be no more than I deserve.'

'You're digging yourself even further into the hole,' she said with some irritation. 'You know I'd never do anything like that. Now, what have you got in mind?'

He pursed his lips, absent-mindedly stroking Charlie's head. 'The next two or three months will be the worst. There's my mother, the job is hard enough, there's a lot of arranging to be done. One possibility is to take leave of absence for a few months till I get myself settled. I want to be with Charlie as much as I can. One bad parent is bad enough. No parents is really rough.'

'We know quite a few successful single parents,' she told him.

A sardonic grin. 'And they're mostly mothers.'

'You can do as much as any mother.' She considered. 'You need to work, though, Toby, and there is the hospital crèche that you could use. Quite a few of our nurses put their children there. But most of them also have some family help—especially from mothers. You know you've got to involve Jack and Carly. There's no need to tell your mother quite yet—get things settled first and I'm sure she'll be thrilled to have a grandson. But when Jack and Carly get roaring mad at you, you've just got to take what they say because it'll be true and it'll be fair.'

'But he's my responsibility and I want to—'

'Toby, you've got to learn to share! That includes sharing your feelings. Have you ever thought how selfish you can be?'

Silence for a while, Then, 'This hasn't been one of the easiest days of my life.'

This was a new Toby. She had never seen him so much in doubt, so unsure of what to do. And with an unexpected surge of feeling she found him more loveable than ever.

Charlie was now drooping over Toby's shoulder, obviously asleep. Toby stood carefully, walked into the bedroom. Annie followed him, watched as Charlie was laid properly on his back, carefully tucked in. There was a gentleness in Toby's handling that made Annie's eyes prickle with tears. This was silly!

She thought back to when they had been together, and she'd casually mentioned having children. He'd said that he wanted to wait until he was forty. And then think about it. A typical joking reply. But, she now realised, with some seriousness as well.

What about herself? She wanted babies, had always wanted to be a mum. In fact, for a while she had thought that she and Toby... She sighed at the memories. It just wasn't fair.

She had to do something so she went into the kitchen and made them both tea. Anything to keep her occupied, while the thoughts and emotions buzzed around her head like bees trapped in a hive.

She took the tea into the living room just as Toby walked in. 'He's fast asleep,' he said. 'Annie, I can't thank you enough for all your help.'

'That's OK. Right, you've now got a week to get used to being a dad, to get to know what to do. I can help you, Toby, and we'll look at what other help you might need. You'd better phone the hospital crèche soon, too.'

Annie was silent for a moment before she asked the question that had been nagging at her since his revelations. 'I need to know,' she said, 'and I suspect you need to tell someone. Who was this woman you were married to for six months?'

At first she thought he wasn't going to answer. And when he did speak his words were curious, rather than bitter. As if he couldn't understand things himself. 'Her name was Gail de Sangrail. If you like, the Honourable Gail de Sangrail. She was as exotic as her name. She was small, blonde, with hair so long she could sit on it.' A definitely bitter smile. 'I think she loved her hair more than she loved me. She was a member of some aristocratic family who have lots of holdings out in the Caribbean. They have pots of money. Gail was training to be a doctor. She was two years behind me. She didn't need to work—for her, medicine was a hobby. And I helped her.'

'And?' Annie wanted to hide her curiosity behind a veil of indifference.

'She was gorgeous, I fell for her and we got married. She insisted that we get married quietly. She didn't want her family—or mine—to know about it. She said we would tell them later. I felt a bit rotten about it, especially later when I decided that she'd wanted a quiet wedding just to spite her mother.'

Annie just couldn't understand this. She knew her own parents' dearest wish was to see her happily married. And to be there at the ceremony. 'So what went wrong?' she asked quietly.

He shrugged. 'I was a toy. And Gail quickly tired of toys. After six months she was thoroughly tired of me and we got a quickie divorce.' He laughed. 'You're not going to believe how tacky it was. We went to Las Vegas and got a divorce there. I told you, Gail's family had plenty of mone. She wanted nothing from me, just wanted me out of her life. She'd lost interest in the medical course, was giving that up. It was the worst time of my life.'

It was hard, but by now Annie was coming to sympathise with him—just a little. His pain was so obvious. She reached across the table, stroked his hand a moment—but then drew back. If she was to be any help at all, she had to be detached. 'Sounds an awful mess,' she said. 'Go on.'

She could see that now he was angry. 'I could have objected, could have tried to fight for what I thought we had. Then I realised I'd be fighting for nothing. Because we had nothing. I'd thought I was in love, I was not. And I decided as we parted that never again would I fall for any woman. I liked them, I liked their company, but never again would I let anyone that close again.'

'It seems a bit hard to judge all women by one,' Annie ventured, 'a bit unfair on half of the human race.'

'True. But it's how I felt. Perhaps how I still feel.'

Annie knew that this meeting was supposed to be about him and his problems. But she still had to ask. 'Is that why you got rid of me, Toby?'

'I was getting very…' He seemed to stumbled over the word. 'I was getting very…fond of you, Annie. But I felt I couldn't give you what you deserved. You never said so, but I knew you wanted love and commitment. It was better for you that I got out of your life.'

'I still think that was a decision I should have been consulted on.' Her voice was frosty. 'But I can see that what you intended was good.' He studied him a moment then asked, 'Am I the only person in this hospital that knows about this?'

'The only one in the city. Apart from a solicitor who acts for me.'

'You've never talked to anyone about it? Not Jack, not Carly, not any of your friends?'

His voice was gruff. 'It was my stupid mistake. Perhaps some silly sense of pride, too. I wanted to forget about it.'

'You don't think that it might have been festering inside you? That it would be good to talk about it—just a little?'

Now he looked uneasy. 'I don't talk about my feelings very much.'

'I've noticed. Toby, I'm not entitled to anything from you. Or perhaps I am. Anyway, I want to know more about your relationship with your wife.'

'Why? Surely it'll only cause you more hurt?'

'There are few greater hurts than being deceived, being kept in the dark, Toby.'

He winced as she went on, 'The hurt is the point. I want to know how you got the way you are. So determined never again to form a long relationship.'

His smile was grim. 'The story doesn't show me in a particularly good light.'

'I'm not sure I see you in a good light anyway,' she said primly. 'You haven't got much to lose.' Then she added, 'And you might gain something.'

He didn't speak at once and she thought back over what she had just said. And felt just a touch ashamed. 'Toby, I sound as if I'm cross-examining you. I'm sorry. But I've just got to know, I want to understand you and if I don't I...well, I'll feel better if I do understand you.'

'Right, then. Gail. Not an uncommon type. First of all, fantastically good-looking. Long hair, peach skin, and the biggest grey eyes. She had this technique of getting close to you—if you were a man, that is. She would hold you, touch you, stare up at you so you were convinced you were the most fascinating man on earth.'

'So how did you fall for this paragon?' Annie felt a little upset by the glowing description.

'I didn't. Well, not at first. I was happy in my own life, busy at work and enjoying it, had the odd girlfriend but in no way was ready to form anything permanent. So when she indicated she wanted to spend a little time with me I wasn't too bothered.'

Toby shook his head, as if unable to believe his own foolishness. 'I remember the exact minute it happened.

She asked me to help her with some work—some genetics, in fact. It was something she didn't quite understand. Her female tutor wasn't very helpful and she'd heard I was good at the subject. It would only take a while and afterwards we might have dinner together. I told her I had a judo tournament.'

Now, apparently, he could smile a little. 'She wasn't very happy about that. Taking second place to a set of sweaty men fighting each other. She'd been rejected. Something she wanted she couldn't have. It couldn't be allowed to happen.'

Toby stood, walked across the room and then sat down again. 'Annie, I still can't understand it when I look back. It was a sort of temporary madness, I was almost hypnotised.'

'So she tried again?' By now Annie was fascinated. It was a story that was both captivating and horrible. And, unfortunately, easy to believe.

'With a bit more success the next time. I have to say she was cunning. Anyway, after a while I thought I was desperately in love and we got married. I did everything she wanted, not even telling my family. I suspect the affair started to fall apart before we even came home from our honeymoon. And when we got divorced I vowed never again to fall for anyone. Annie, I'd tried so hard!'

'Not every woman is like that,' Annie ventured.

'I know that. My brain tells me that's true. Unfortunately, I don't feel it. Whenever I think I might want to commit myself, something stops me.'

'And so you've been happy jumping from woman to woman ever since?'

'Happy enough.'

'You said that you felt almost hypnotised by Gail. Ever thought that that's how some of your women friends might think that that's what you've done to them?'

There was the longest pause ever. 'That's a hard accusation,' he said. And she knew he was upset.

'Perhaps you'll change now,' she suggested. 'Who knows? You might be happier.'

She put her arms round him, pulled him to her. It was meant to be nothing more than a hug. Then she kissed him. 'This is a kiss from a friend to another friend,' she said. 'You need comfort, that's all.' But as she kissed him she remembered how things had been between them. It would be so easy... She pushed him away, firmly but gently.

'If you need me, I can stay,' she said. 'You've got a spare bedroom. D'you want me to stay? To help you with Charlie?'

Toby smiled. 'I'd love you to. Thanks, Annie.'

CHAPTER FIVE

SHE slept well. The past two days had been hard work, she needed rest. But she still woke up quite early.

She had been up once already, Charlie was sleeping in Toby's room and had screamed at three in the morning. Annie had heard the noise, had pulled on the dressing-gown that Toby had lent her and had gone to help him. Charlie needed a drink and a cuddle. Three o'clock in the morning, both she and Toby in his bedroom, very aware that they were naked under their dressing-gowns. Though it hadn't worried either of them. Annie grinned sourly as she remembered an old midwife telling her, 'There's no finer contraceptive than a baby.'

She switched on the bedside light, put on the dressing-gown again. It smelled evocatively of Toby and despite her churned-up emotions, she had to fight the urge to bury her face in it.

In the middle of the living room table was a note. *Charlie and I have gone to fetch breakfast. Stay in bed.*

Fetch breakfast? Stay in bed? Well, it would be impolite not to do as he suggested, so she went back to bed.

A short while later she heard the front door open, then he knocked on her bedroom door about ten minutes afterwards. By now she was almost used to the jerk of excitement that juddered through her. Would she ever lose this reaction? She thought probably not. He came in and stood there, holding a gurgling Charlie in his arms, and Annie felt her heart twist at the sight.

'We thought you might like some breakfast, maybe as a little thank you,' said Toby. 'So we've been to the supermarket.'

'At this time? In the middle of the morning? Even after he got us both up?'

He nodded. 'I thought I might as well fetch us something exciting for breakfast.'

'You know that all I have is tea for breakfast. Porridge in winter, cereals in summer.'

'I know. But just for once we're going continental. Coffee then hot croissants and a fruit compote. And you're to have them in bed.'

She gave in and smiled. 'It'll make a change,' she said. 'Quite a nice change, too.'

While he was out of the room she shook her head in bewilderment. How her life had changed in the past few hours. And the future—who could tell? Was she happy? Well, she thought, at least life wasn't boring. Then she thought of the ancient Chinese curse, 'May you live in interesting times.' Times were certainly interesting to her now.

'So how are you getting on with Charlie?' she asked

when he came back in, minus his son. 'Did you enjoy the trip out?'

He shook his head, as if mystified. 'He was as good as gold. D'you know, yesterday, when I saw Charlie for the first time, I was just shell-shocked. But now I've had a sleep. And this morning I looked at him and everything clicked into place. Thanks to you as well, mind. He's my son and I love him with a strength I didn't know I had.'

Annie felt her eyes prickling as he said that. She'd always suspected Toby capable of vast love. Now she knew it. A pity even a little of it wasn't directed towards her. 'So what are you going to do about it?' she asked.

'Whatever Charlie needs, he'll get. And the first thing is a family. Tonight he can meet Uncle Jack and Auntie Carly. It's the right time.'

'Looking forward to the meeting?'

'Not entirely. I've half a mind to throw little Charlie into the fray first, so that they can fall in love with him and will have cooled down before I have to say my piece.'

'Miranda will be on your side,' Annie said with a grin, 'and I bet Charlie will have a cousin within a year or so.'

'I hope so. Now, I think I can smell the coffee. Be back in a moment.'

I like this new Toby, Annie thought. It's a side of him I've never quite seen before. All that love! Then she felt a bit guilty. If he was capable of feeling, showing so much love—why hadn't some come her way? She understood he had to concentrate entirely on Charlie now—but wasn't there room somewhere for her, too? She sighed.

He came back into the bedroom, placed a tray on her lap and sat on the edge of the bed with his own tray. The coffee smelt wonderful and the hot rolls were heaven, too.

'I could get used to this,' she said, then realised that perhaps she had said too much.

Perhaps he had been reading her mind. 'You were so good to me yesterday, Annie.'

She looked at him with some irritation. 'It wasn't a case of me being good to you, Toby. I was being good to Charlie, too.'

He stretched out his arm, stroked her shoulder and she tried to hide the great pleasure this simple act gave her. 'I just want you to know that I think you're marvellous and if things were different I—'

Harshly she said, 'Things aren't different, so listen. You've got problems and I'm willing to do something to help. No, I want to help. Have you thought more about how you're going to manage work and caring for Charlie? About the future?'

He pushed his hand through his hair. 'Nothing in a hurry. I've got a week to decide, to plan a future. First, as I said, is Jack and Carly. I'll ask and listen. But one thing is certain. This is *my* problem. I'm grateful for your help—I know I need it—but I'm not expecting it or taking it for granted.'

Silence for a moment. Annie looked at the bedside clock and said, 'I'd better go to work. I've just got time to get to my place, shower and change.' She smiled. 'Now get out of here while I pull on some clothes.'

Perhaps she understood him a little better now, she

thought after he'd left and she was getting dressed. She didn't feel quite so angry at him for dumping her the way he had. She considered that and then decided that, yes, she did still feel angry. But perhaps a bit less so. She was certainly no Gail, anyway, and he should have been able to realise that.

The following morning Annie walked down the clinic corridor and saw Eva talking to Mary and…Toby. What was he doing there? Where was Charlie?

Toby called her over and he, Eva and Mary smiled at her. Annie found herself feeling a bit warm, a bit uncomfortable. Almost as if the fact that she'd stayed at Toby's was blazoned on her forehead. Perhaps people could tell just by her expression. But if they could, they kept it quiet.

She was told that although he had been given leave of absence, Toby had been asked to come in just for the morning session due to a staff shortage. So what had he done with Charlie?

'I've been asked to cancel both yours and Toby's appointments this morning,' Eva said. 'There's a bit of a crisis over in the main building. Too many people off sick again so we've been asked if you can do a ward round together. Just this once. It's paediatrics, not obs and gynae, but I doubt there'll be much trouble. Mary here says she can cope with your visits and there's nothing much else that can't be put off.'

'No problem,' said Annie. Technically they both should be doing a lot of donkey work on the wards, having to run their own clinic was a step up. Every now and again it was as well to do the work they were supposed to do.

They walked over to the main building together. 'So where's Charlie?' she asked.

'In a local crèche,' he said. 'I didn't want gossip to spread before I tell the family, so managed to get some recommendations for crèches outside the hospital without giving the game away. When I explained the situation to the people there they were more then willing to help. I didn't want to leave him, but I'm needed here and at least it's just for the morning. He should be OK.'

He then told her that he had made more phone calls, arranging a meeting that evening with Jack and Carly.

'Good luck,' she told him. 'You're going to need it.'

He seemed just a little low. 'I'm not the favourite brother,' he explained. 'Jack and Carly expected me at my mother's last night, I phoned in with an obvious excuse. Arranging the meeting was a bit fraught, too. They wanted to know what it was about and I wouldn't tell them.'

'It'll be all right later. When they see Charlie. Toby, you're lucky to have a brother and sister.'

They walked down a long corridor, turned into Kingfisher Ward. 'I've got problems,' he said. 'But the kids here have even bigger problems. At least Charlie is healthy. Kind of puts things into perspective.' And the old Toby smile was back.

Kingfisher Ward. The ward for the less seriously ill children. Annie liked the room. There were bright pictures on the walls. There was a play corner, full of different toys. Fastened to a giant corkboard, in clear plastic folders, were the children's own paintings. They got to take them home when they left. The staff prided themselves on the relaxed, family atmosphere of the cheerful ward.

Six-year-old Martin Track was certain of two things. One, he wasn't ill; two, he wasn't going to be examined. There might have been a third thing, that he was going to cause as much havoc as possible. Annie didn't know.

In fact, Martin had had recurrent tonsillitis, caused by the Epstein-Barr virus, and had finally had his tonsils removed. It wasn't a serious operation and Martin should have gone home after a one-night stay. But he had been bleeding a little and there were family problems. So Martin had to stay in hospital. He didn't like it, he didn't like people peering into his mouth, and his objections could upset the entire ward.

'Now for a struggle,' the nurse said as they approached Martin's bed. Martin stared at them balefully.

'Look Martin,' Toby said, and extended an open hand. In the middle of his palm was a red sweet. 'Would you like it?'

Martin nodded.

Toby closed his fingers, opened them at once. Martin stared at the palm, then reached out to turn Toby's hand over. No red sweet.

'We'll have to think about this,' grumbled Toby. He

closed his hand again, shook it in the air. When he opened it there was a sweet—a yellow one.

'I wanted a red one, I really did,' said Toby. 'Didn't you?'

'Yes.' Martin was now intrigued.

Toby sat on the edge of the bed. 'Let's see where it's got to,' he said. 'It might have gone to all sorts of odd places. Just sit up and let Annie here take off your pyjama jacket.' He nodded to the Annie who whipped off the jacket. 'Now,' Toby went on, 'while she's looking at you, we'll look for the red sweetie.'

Annie managed all the obs that were necessary. And the search for the red sweet went on. A brown one was found inside one of Martin's ears. A green one even appeared from his nose—to much laughter from the little boy. It was magic!

Obs were quickly over. They left a puzzled but happy Martin rubbing his ears and then inspecting his hands. 'That's the quietest I've ever seen him,' said the nurse. 'You were great.'

'Where did you learn to do that?' Annie asked.

He shrugged. 'A couple of years ago we had a conjurer come to a ward I was working on, to entertain the kids at Christmas. I saw him do that trick and I asked him to show me how to do it. He was a good guy—it was a professional secret but he showed me. I practised it—and on a children's ward it's as useful as a stethoscope.'

'Right,' said Annie, impressed with his resourcefulness.

'For kids, the world can be full of magic,' he went on. 'It's real for them. I want Charlie to grow up in a world of magic.'

'And then learn what life is really like?' Annie couldn't help being a little bitter.

'Sometimes adults can find magic in their lives, too.' But he didn't tell her how.

Toby got on with all the children. He seemed to treat them as if they were adults—and they liked it. Annie couldn't quite explain how he did it, but it worked. And as he entertained them, she managed to get the work done.

'We're a good team, Annie,' he said. 'We work well together.'

It was true.

Three-quarters of the way through the ward round, the nurse looked at the entrance and shivered. 'Here comes trouble. Mrs Everett. Her little girl is quiet and placid, and a perfect patient. She must take after her father, because Mrs Everett's never happy unless she's finding fault.'

Parents were encouraged to spend as much time on the ward as possible. It helped the children recover. Whenever Annie looked around the ward there would be a few parents, helping not only their own child but others, too. Usually they were mothers, but there was a steadily increasing number of fathers, too.

Toby looked cautiously at the thin-lipped Mrs Everett. 'D'you think she'd respond to the sweetie trick Annie?' he whispered. 'Or will she need chocolate or something?'

'I think you might have your work cut out here,' Annie murmured. 'It'll take more than sweets to win her over.'

Toby grinned. 'Whatever it takes, I'll see if I've got it. You two carry on with the round. I'll get a cup of tea for Mrs Everett.'

Annie and the nurse watched him walk across the ward, saw his broad smile, heard him call, 'Mrs Everett, I don't think we've met yet. I'm Dr Sinclair and it's nice to meet you. Let me get you a drink.'

'I don't think I've ever said it before,' said the nurse, 'but in this case I'm really pleased to see a doctor drinking tea when he should be doing his rounds.'

Annie saw the two sitting in the parents' glass-walled room, saw Toby fetch tea for a smiling Mrs Everett. She nodded. 'Toby can be a real charmer. We all know that.'

It was a good ward round and it was over quite quickly. They both had to go back to the clinic and as they did so Toby said, 'It's true, you know. We work well together. We're a good team.'

'We're a good team of doctors,' said Annie.

As she walked down to her room she thought about what she had just said. They were a good team of doctors. They could anticipate each other, guess what the other was thinking. It was a pity that they had so much difficulty with their personal lives.

Back to the clinic for the inevitable paperwork. Toby had an hour before he went to pick up Charlie. Time to catch up a little. So they sat together in the staff lounge, working their way through mounds of files and requisitions and patient reports. Toby's presence made the seemingly endless task seem quite pleasant.

'Dr Arnold,' he said gloomily after half an hour, 'I feel in need of surgical division of a compression ligament.'

'You feel in need of what?'

'I shall also need a letter from my doctor certifying that I am unfit for work and will remain that way for the foreseeable future. You can be my doctor.'

'Toby, what are you talking about?'

He flapped his hand up and down in front of her. 'I have carpal tunnel syndrome. Pain and tingling in the fingers. Caused by an excess of handwriting. Writing up notes, to be exact. I just can't stand the pain, Doctor.'

'There's a new, certain, instant cure,' Annie said laconically. 'A hot infusion of caffeine, sucrose and lactose. And while you're on your feet, I'll have a coffee, too.'

He shook his head as he got to his feet. 'I ask for sympathy and I'm turned into a domestic drudge. Life just isn't fair.'

This was the Toby that Annie liked, the one she felt she knew, could get on with. There might be another Toby somewhere—but that one was dangerous.

Eva popped her head round the door. 'Message from your mother,' she said to Annie. 'Can you phone her— some time latish this afternoon? Not now, she's just going out.'

'Thanks, Eva. I'll remember to do that.'

'You know quite a bit about my family,' Toby said

casually, as he flipped through his papers. 'I know nothing about yours. Tell me a bit.'

Annie shrugged. 'Not a lot to tell. We're just an ordinary, happy family. My dad's a retired bank manager, my mother's a part-time school helper, and they live in a semi in Lancaster. We're a very small family. I'm an only child.'

'Do you see a lot of them?'

'Not as much as I ought to. Of course, work has been a bit pressing recently. In fact, probably my mother's phoning me to ask why I haven't been home for tea.'

She worked for another five minutes and then looked at the pile of papers in front of her with considerable satisfaction. 'That's done. Paperwork over for at least three days. Now I can pretend I am a doctor.'

'I haven't finished,' Toby complained. 'It's your fault, I've had to spend much of my time fetching you coffee. Will you do some of mine?'

'No,' said Annie. But after a moment she said, 'Well, pass a few easy ones over. If you want to go now and see how Charlie's getting on, that's all right with me. I'll finish your paperwork.'

'It'd be nice to go now,' he said. 'Thanks.' Then he said hesitantly, 'Are you...will you be calling later?'

'I'll bring something over for your tea,' she said. 'See you then.'

He came over, kissed her on the forehead. She'd like more than that, she thought. But she said nothing.

Time to leave the clinic. Annie had food in her own flat she could pick up, no need to go shopping. But there was something else she needed to do before she arrived at Toby's flat. She had a decision to make. She hurried down the corridor, stopped long enough to pick up her mac. It had started to rain.

Outside it was dark, there was a bitter wind blowing the rain across the hospital grounds. There was nobody around, just what she wanted. She walked along a path, the rain pattering on her coat. In the distance she could see the blurred lights of the hospital; they seemed strangely distant. Good. She needed solitude.

Eventually she found a tree and sheltered against its trunk. No one could see her. She needed for a while to be absolutely alone, to make a decision she had been considering all day. It might be a foolish decision.

These recent days had been the most tumultuous of her life. She had discovered her true feelings for Toby; she had discovered he was a father; she had been given some explanation for why he had treated her so badly. Her whole life felt as if it had been turned upside down. And now she was contemplating an even bigger change, one that would hopefully get her life back on track once and for all. For a moment she thought of her mother, who she intended to speak to later that night. One of her ambitions had always been to have a married life as contented as her parents'. She suspected that she was about to embark on a plan that was just the opposite of their clearly laid out path.

She thought a moment longer. Then she hurried back before she changed her mind.

* * *

Charlie had been fine at the crèche and Toby was delighted. His son was now asleep and he and Annie were sitting at the living-room table, having finished the frozen casserole that Annie had brought. Toby was looking just a little more relaxed. And Annie was feeling anxious. What she was about to suggest would affect her entire life. She wasn't sure whether it was a good decision or not.

'Toby? You know my rotation is up in two months? Well, I was intending to stay here, if they'd have me. But now I've changed my mind. It might be good to have experience of a totally different hospital. In fact, Calvin has said that he'll see if he can find me a place in America for a while.'

Toby looked up, obviously upset. 'But why? The training you get here is second to none.' He thought a moment and asked, 'Is it because of me? Because if I thought I'd driven you out, I wouldn't be able to live with myself. And I'm feeling bad enough already.'

'It's partly about you,' she said honestly, 'but there are other reasons. Now, listen to what else I've got to say. You're going to have to see to Charlie. You said you might even stop your course for a while. I think that would be a foolish thing to do. The hospital crèche will take Charlie during a lot of the day. But apart from that, what Jack and Carly can do for you is limited. So I'm making you an offer.'

She stopped, conscious that this was her last chance to change her mind. Then she took a deep breath and said, 'I'm making you an offer. For two months I'll share looking after Charlie with you. I'll keep my own flat going but I'll move in here with you. Charlie can go to the hospital crèche during the day. We can ask John Bennett not to schedule the two of us on night duty at the same time. Some nights I'll have Charlie, some nights you'll have him. And there'll be the mornings, of course. It shouldn't be too hard for the two of us. But only for two months. After that he's your responsibility.'

He looked at her unbelievingly. 'You'd do that for me? Why?'

'My reasons are my own. Perhaps I just like babies.'

She could see he was thinking, almost at a loss for words. Recently he seemed to have been getting more shocks than he'd ever had in his life. She saw glimpses of a different Toby, one who could feel and show his feelings. And she liked this different Toby.

He muttered, 'That's generosity beyond belief. And I know I don't deserve it.' Then he shook his head, as if to rid it of distracting thoughts. His voice was firmer. 'Will you be able to let go of Charlie after two months? You know you'll grow fond of him.'

'Let's be quite clear about this. After two months I'm going. You'll be on your own or I suppose you'll find a nanny or something. I'm a doctor. I've been fond of children before and they've left me. It'll be hard but I've done harder things. I've had to.'

He stood, came over to her and taking her two hands in his, stared into her eyes. She stared back, making herself feel strong. 'We'll be spending a lot of time together, Annie. Will you be able to leave me after two months?'

Her gaze didn't waver. 'Yes. I've done it before, remember? I've had to. And one thing, Toby, from you

I want the most solemn promise that you understand that after two months it's all over.'

He squeezed her hands. 'I don't deserve you or your offer,' he said. 'Of course I accept. I've got to do everything I can for Charlie. I'd like to think that if it was just for me, I'd have the courage to refuse. But I doubt it.'

They looked at each other in silence. Then she pulled free her hands and said, 'My offer might not be needed. Perhaps Jack and Carly will have another suggestion. Incidentally, it's time you were on your way to see them.'

Toby nodded. 'I'm avoiding the issue,' he said after a minute. 'I know that I should go and get changed, and take Charlie to see my brother and sister. But the more I think about facing the family, the more inviting staying here with you becomes. D'you think I'm a coward, Annie?'

'Definite white-feather material.' She glanced at her watch. 'If you don't leave this building in the twenty minutes, I'll kick you out.'

'Come with me?'

'No. You've got to take it on the chin alone.' She grinned. 'Just one thing. Get Miranda on your side.'

'I'm going,' he said. 'Give you a report when I get back.'

Annie watched him leave. Had she done the most stupid thing in her life?

Toby drove slowly to Jack's house and thought of Annie's offer. He wasn't a fool, he knew what she felt for him. In fact, he suspected that he understood what she felt better than she did herself.

He wished he had treated her better. He wished that he would be able to treat her better. But he knew he couldn't give her what she wanted—pure, simple, total love. He'd been in love once. Or he'd thought he'd been in love. It had lasted barely six months. He was not going to make that mistake again.

There had been other women since, casual affairs, a clear understanding on both sides that it had just been a fun thing. None of them had meant very much to him. Only Annie had managed to get under his iron carapace, to make him feel that perhaps here was a woman who he could imagine spending his life with. And so he'd had to give her up. He'd tried that once already.

But now this new situation. He had promised himself he wouldn't hurt Annie and he strongly suspected that living with him would hurt her. It would hurt him, too. But he was not going to hurt Annie. Not again. He'd turn down her offer. He'd manage somehow.

He drove on—but slowly.

He was headed for his meeting with the family, Charlie was with him. And as he drove he glanced down at the little face illuminated by the passing flashing lights. A feeling stronger than any he'd ever know washed over him. This was his son! He had to do the best he could for him, had to think of him first. So he would accept Annie's offer. He knew it would be the better for Charlie. But he would be fair to her. At the end of two months he would see that she could leave without recriminations. He owed her that.

CHAPTER SIX

IRONING was good for the soul, Annie decided. It might be wearying for the body but it was good for the soul. She pressed her hands against the small of her back, stretched painfully. She looked with doubtful pride at the now empty plastic basket to one side of her and the double pile of freshly ironed clothes on the table at the other side. A good job well done. She wouldn't need to do any ironing for weeks now.

She had gone back to her own flat for a couple of hours. She could manage to be happy in Toby's flat when he and Charlie were there. But when she was alone there—imagining what life would be like if she were there permanently—it was too painful.

Perhaps her flat was looking a little, well, not grubby but uncared-for. Time for a quick zip round with the vacuum cleaner, some cushion plumping and then a bit of polishing. Only when she found herself starting to polish the table for a second time did she realise what she was doing. This was all displacement activity. She was trying to take her mind off Toby and Charlie.

They had made no more plans when he'd left to take Charlie to meet his new relations. But she knew that he'd want to involve her. Then again, suppose he didn't want to involve her? What would happen if, after talking to Jack and Carly, he decided he didn't need her help at all? Annie blinked. She'd never even considered that. But he must need her, her help would be invaluable, and besides, she needed... *She* needed? Was this about her needs?

The phone rang. And she realised that this was what she had been expecting.

It was Miranda and she sounded cheerful, excited. 'It's good to be able to talk to someone normal,' she said. 'Someone not like my family-to-be.' But there was laughter in her voice.

'Aren't Jack and Carly and Toby normal?' Annie asked.

'Well, I never knew they could all get so irate. But we've all cooled down now. Charlie's smoothed things over. Charlie is a darling.' Miranda's voice lowered. 'Look, I gather you've made an offer to help Toby and we'd all like to talk to you about it. I was going to phone and ask you to come round. Jack said no way, if you wanted to come we'd pick you up. So do you want to come?'

Annie could feel her heart beating quickly again. She had made a decision and she was being drawn ever more deeply into its consequences. Soon it would be impossible to back out. So what? She didn't intend to back out. 'I'd love to come round, but I can drive.'

'No chance. Apart from anything else, I want a private word with you myself. I'll be there in fifteen minutes.' Miranda rang off.

* * *

Being engaged suited Miranda. Annie could see the happiness glowing in her, see it in her smile, hear it in her voice. And she wondered if she'd ever feel happiness like that herself. She hoped so.

'We'll drive slowly,' Miranda announced. 'We've got things to talk about. Annie, I'm talking as your friend, not as a member of the Sinclair clan. Now, Toby told us of the offer you made him. You tell me what you said.'

'I said I'd share the looking after of Charlie for the next two months, just to give Toby time to get his life organised. Just two months. Then I'll disappear out of his life.'

'I don't want you to disappear out of his life. It means you'll disappear out of mine, and you're my friend.' Miranda's voice got sharper. 'What's in this for you, Annie? I thought you'd got over Toby, but this means you'll be tossed into the deep end again. Any feelings you used to have for him are likely to come back.'

Annie's voice was flat. 'Too late. They're back already.'

Miranda sighed, said nothing for a moment. 'Oh, Annie! Are you hoping that living with him will bring him round to seeing what he threw away?'

'No. I'm just going to stay with him to help him with Charlie. Toby's been completely thrown in at the deep end and, as a friend, I want to make sure he and Charlie will be OK.'

'It'll be hell for you!'

'Perhaps so. But it'll be a hell I have chosen for myself.'

Miranda shook her head in dismay. 'It's got to be your decision. But if you ever want to back out, I'll support you.'

Annie ruffled Miranda's hair. 'It's good to have friends,' she said. 'And that's what I'm trying to be.'

Annie had been to Jack's flat before; she thought it was wonderful. It showed a side of his character that didn't always come out when he was at work. It showed that Jack loved beauty.

The family was sitting in a circle in the living room. There was Toby, looking tired but relieved. Carly was cuddling Charlie and apparently really enjoying it. Jack looked sardonic.

As Annie looked at them together, she could see the family resemblance. They all had different faces but there was something about the determined line of the jaws, the bone structure round the eyes. They were a handsome family, with the kind of good looks that that would last into middle age.

She could also feel the family togetherness. Toby could rely on them, and for a moment Annie felt almost excluded. What need did Toby have of her, when his siblings were on his side?

Jack came over to her, kissed her on the cheek. 'We're having a drink,' he said. 'It's a bit late but this is an occasion for celebration. We've got a new member of the family.'

He turned to a silver bucket on a side table, filled a glass with champagne and handed it to her. 'Same toast as before,' he said. 'To Charlie!'

They all lifted their glasses. 'To Charlie!'

'I think he's a wonderful little lad,' said Annie.

She sat in the seat Jack offered her, next to himself. She was opposite Toby. He picked up his own chair and carried it round to sit next to her, She liked the symbolism of that. But they were not really together, were they? Or not for long.

'Toby has told us about your offer to help him,' Jack said, 'and we all think that's wonderful of you. We'll leave it up to you two to organise. What we wanted to say was that Carly, Miranda, myself, we can't do as much as we would like. You know how our mother is ill, every morning one of us calls in to see her briefly, at least one of us sits with her every night. She can't say much but we know she knows we are there, and she appreciates it. But…this can't go on for much longer.'

'I know how things are,' said Annie, 'and if it were my mother I'd feel exactly the same. It's no big thing I'm offering Toby. And it's only for a couple of months. But it'll give him time to really settle with Charlie. You know I've made it very clear that I can only help for two months?'

Jack nodded. 'It's a good idea to get things clearly set out to begin with. Now, I've always been against using any influence I might have in hospital to help family members, but I feel I can ask John Bennett to arrange that you two don't, for example, have to work nights together. Another glass, Annie?'

'Please,' said Annie.

'We need to move fast,' Toby said by her side. 'I've been talking to Miranda, our resident expert midwife. She's given me a list of what I'll need. I'll get it ordered tomorrow. I told you, midwives know stuff that doctors don't. And for a start I'm soon going to need another place to live, my flat just isn't big enough. Give me a hand looking at places, Annie?'

'Yes,' said Annie, 'I guess so.' She had the feeling that she had started sliding down a helter-skelter, there was no way she could get back now, and the further she slid, the faster she went. And while it was exhilarating, it was a bit frightening, too.

'There's something else you have to think of,' Miranda said. 'There's no way to keep this quiet. Two SHOs and a sudden baby? The pair of you have got to find something to announce. Or Lord knows what the gossips will say.'

Annie flinched but she knew what Miranda said was true.

'What do you think, Annie?' Toby's voice was concerned. 'I've given up worrying about what people think about me, but you have a reputation to consider.'

What did she want? At the moment she just couldn't think. 'We've got a week or two to decide on a story,' she said eventually. 'I suppose we could decide to hide nothing. Just tell the truth.'

'Now, that would be original,' said Miranda.

It was getting late, it had been a full day. Toby drove them back to his own flat. She had said that her stay could start at once.

'I'll say it once again,' he said as she climbed out of his car. 'I want you to know just how much I appreciate this. I've had a bit of time to think and now I know just how much it is that you're offering me. And I'm not accepting for myself, but for Charlie. But if ever you want to back out…'

She leaned forward, kissed him quickly on the cheek. 'If I want to back out, you'll be the first to know.'

She was tired—exhausted even. But she knew she wouldn't sleep at once. She had a hot bath in Toby's bathroom, took herself to bed with the usual warm drink and sat up to think about her day. And about her future.

Earlier she had thought she was on a helter-skelter. Now she realised that a better image might be an emotional roller-coaster. First she had discovered that she still loved him, but was not sure what to do about it. They had become friends; he seemed quite happy to remain that way. Then she'd found out about Charlie. At first she had been confused, hurting, angry. But then she'd seen Toby holding his son, had seen the love he felt for him. It was almost more than she could bear, seeing him with a child that so easily could have been their child.

When she'd learned about Toby's unhappy marriage she'd thought that she could understand—just—why he'd dumped her just when she'd thought she'd found the love of her life. She couldn't forget but she could understand. And she felt that this gave her permission to love Toby even more.

So she had made her offer. She had convinced herself that she had made it because someone she loved was in need and trouble. That she was being a friend, just as she'd told Miranda. But she had to be ruthlessly honest. She knew that a tiny corner of her mind hoped that eventually, after spending so much time with her, Toby would come to realise that he couldn't live without her, that he loved her. But she knew it was foolish to hope.

With this recognition came a kind of peace. She turned off her bedside light and was almost instantly asleep.

It was almost a relief next morning to do some simple medicine. She had a clinic, saw a variety of mums and babies with a variety of problems. Most of them were reasonably easy to deal with. At the end of the morning Annie felt pleased with her life. She had helped people; she was doing what a doctor should.

Tony hadn't come in for coffee in the midmorning break. He'd put his head round the door, winked at her and said, 'Can't stop but I'll see you at one.' And then he had gone. But he had seemed different, had looked at her in a different way as if they…belonged to each other? There had been something in his face as he'd smiled at her, as if they shared some kind of happy secret. Well, that was what she felt. She wondered if he felt the same.

She knew Toby was a good doctor. She'd been impressed by the casual but efficient way he'd dealt with the running of their little clinic. She hadn't quite realised what a skilful organiser he was.

At one o'clock he told her, 'I've got an appointment to see the sister in charge of the crèche here. I'm going to order the stuff that Miranda suggested and have it delivered. Then I've got to see a solicitor about Charlie. I need to know where we stand legally with his grandmother. I don't want her suddenly turning up, demanding him back.'

'She is his relation,' Annie suggested gently. 'You need to tread carefully here, for Charlie's sake.'

Toby's voice was harsh. 'When he's old enough I'm sure he'll be curious about them. When he can make up his own mind, I'll be pleased if he wants to go to see them. I know what he'll think. But until then, he's staying with me.'

Annie surveyed him. 'Even four days ago you were a lot more…more easygoing than you are now,' she said. 'You're losing that casual Toby attitude. You seem to…to care more about things.'

He sighed. 'Being a parent does that to you. It makes you think more clearly, realise the consequences of your actions. But I'm still the same Toby underneath.'

To prove it, he smiled the old Toby smile. 'Bye, Annie. I'll not see you till late tonight but we'll make more arrangements tomorrow. I'm taking Charlie to Jack's for a couple of hours so the family can get to know their nephew.' And he was gone.

Annie sighed when he had gone. 'Realise the consequences of your actions indeed.' He had a few more lessons to learn. But what an awful lot she had learned about Toby Sinclair in the past few days. And she realised that what she had learned had made her love him more than ever.

* * *

Annie and Toby only worked for three days a week in their clinic. The other days they spent either in SHO classes or working as they had before, in the wards, clinics or delivery rooms of the main hospital.

Next day Annie was working in the main hospital. She was on duty in Nightingale Ward, one of the children's wards. This was not a cheerful place, like Kingfisher Ward, often full of laughter and occasionally mischief. It was an intensive care unit where the sickest of children were nursed.

It turned out to be one of Annie's worst ever days. And there was no Toby around to help her, to comfort her or cheer her up. He could be such a support to her, she hadn't realised just how much she had come to rely on his casual good humour.

Annie walked into the clinic just at handover, when the leaving staff briefed the incoming staff. And she could feel the atmosphere at once.

She knew what it was. 'Baby Caroline?' she asked the SHO going off duty. She remembered the case from last week.

He nodded. 'She started to slip away early this morning. I phoned for John Bennett, he came out, but everyone knew there was nothing that could be done. Her parents are with her in the side ward. It won't be long now.'

Baby Caroline had Edwards' syndrome, a rare condition affecting one in every five thousand babies. She had an extra eighteenth chromosome. She had been born with heart, lung and digestive problems. Jack had operated to correct the abnormalities of the heart. At first it had been thought that there might be some hope, perhaps she had a fighting chance. For a while she had lived at home. But then her condition had deteriorated and she had been readmitted. And the consultants had had to admit defeat.

Annie went along to let the parents know she was there. They knew that no medical attention could help now, but it was courteous to know she was available. The nursing staff would look after them, do all that was necessary.

A side ward, room for just one incubator. Curtains drawn across the windows that opened into the main ward. Two chairs drawn up, baby Caroline's parents sitting there, staring numbly at their dying child.

'Mr and Mrs Godwin, I'm so sorry. I'm running a clinic next door so I'll be there or on the ward all afternoon. If there's anything at all that I can do, please, send a nurse for me.'

'Thank you, Doctor,' Mrs Godwin said. 'The nurses are looking after us and…and…Caroline very well.'

That was it. There was nothing more to be said.

With a heavy heart, Annie went to begin her antenatal clinic, forcing herself to look cheerful. She couldn't run the clinic with an unhappy face. There were women facing coming births; each had a different attitude. Some were elated, just couldn't wait. Others were by now thoroughly fed up with the discomfort. More than a few were apprehensive—even frightened. So this visit was more than just a check-up on their physical state. Annie had to listen, to understand, to sympathise. She couldn't do that looking miserable.

But as she smiled and dealt with each case in turn, there was always a bitter comparison at the back of her mind. These women were looking forward to a baby being born. Not too far away a couple was waiting for their baby to die.

Sometimes being a doctor was hard.

In fact, it happened when she was in the staff lounge, drinking coffee and wishing she had Toby there to cheer her up. The staff nurse in charge opened the door, said nothing, just looked at her. Annie nodded and put down her coffee.

Caroline's parents were now in the staff nurse's office. The little side ward held two empty chairs and an incubator.

Only a doctor could pronounce death. No need for a long examination. Annie signed the forms that were held out to her. The rest would be left to the nursing staff.

The work of the clinic had to go on. But the knowledge of the death seemed to spread a blight over the building. The staff carried on with their work, smiled and joked when it was necessary. But voices seemed a little muted.

Annie drove back to her flat. She felt tired. She had the usual bath and then sat on the couch with the usual hot drink. The living room was spotless, she thought of yesterday's orgy of cleaning and smiled wearily. How to deal with an excess of emotion. Clean things! She was too tired to clean anything now.

It was Caroline's death that was hurting her. She'd been through this before. She was a doctor; she had to tread that thin line between feeling and detachment. It was right and proper to feel sympathy for your patients. It made you a better doctor. But you could not share in all their grief. There were so many patients, so much pain, distress and death. You had to accept that, do what you could but be well aware that you could not do too much. Still, it was hard. Especially when it was a child who died.

Then she realised. She was thinking of the new baby in her life. She was thinking of Charlie—and Toby. And somehow Charlie had connected with Caroline. He was a baby, he was vulnerable. He too could…

She'd left the ward in a hurry. It might have been better if she'd gone with a couple of the nurses to the Red Lion. She needed someone to talk to, to share her feelings with.

Toby would be ideal.

They weren't to meet again until late this evening when she went round to his flat. He was going to take Charlie to see Carly. But Annie wanted to be with him now. He wouldn't have set off for Carly's yet, so she could phone him for a chat. She picked up her phone, put it down. Let him have some peace. Then she picked up the phone and rang his number. She was doing something for him. He could do something for her. All she wanted was a friendly couple of words.

'Annie, good to hear from you. How's things?' His voice was warm and friendly; he seemed genuinely pleased that she had called.

'Everything's fine. I just wondered how you got on today.'

She had tried to keep her voice cheerful but evidently she hadn't succeeded. She could hear the concern in his voice when he asked, 'Is everything all right, Annie? You sound a bit…unhappy? You know, if you're having second thoughts about our arrangement I—'

'It's not that. I want to look after Charlie. It's just that I did my stint on Nightingale Ward and Caroline…' Her voice trailed away.

He knew at once. 'She died. I'm sorry. We've been expecting it, Annie, but it's always a shock.' He was silent a minute and then went on. 'It's a terrible thing to say but I feel more understanding now I have my own child. I really didn't know what I was talking about before.'

'Exactly,' she said.

He was silent again. Then, 'It happens,' he said. 'We're taught to distance ourselves when we see people ill or dying. We're taught to be sympathetic but not get too involved. And mostly we manage that. But every now and again a case comes along where it just doesn't work. You know it's foolish to feel but you just do. Is that the way you feel about Caroline?'

'That's the way,' she said, grateful that Toby understood exactly how she was feeling. How well he seemed to know her…

'Look, Annie, Charlie and I are going round to Carly's tonight. I didn't invite you because, well, because you're doing so much for us already. I thought you might need time to yourself. But you know Carly would be delighted to see you. And so would I.'

'No, Toby, I can't do that. You go and—'

'Can you hear that knocking at your front door?' he interrupted.

'No!'

'Well, it's Charlie and me. Or if it isn't, it will be in about fifteen minutes.'

He arrived with Charlie in exactly fifteen minutes. She let him in without speaking and then moved back to her couch and just sat there.

He seemed to divine her mood. He said nothing himself, just made her a mug of tea. They sat side by side on her couch, drinking tea.

After a moment, with a gentle hand he started to stroke her hair. 'Toby…' She tried to move her head away.

'I'll stop if you want.' He didn't stop and she said nothing. And after a while she found it soothing. Her breathing calmed back to normal. She took a tissue from her desk, wiped her tears, blew her nose. Then, still silently, she fetched them both some more tea and offered him one of her biscuits.

He didn't say anything, for which she was glad. Just the gentle regular stroking of her hair.

In their short affair they had been many things to each other. Their passion had blazed and then been extinguished. They had become friends and now she had agreed—in the weirdest way—to become a foster-parent to his child. But there had never been occasion for him to be kind, to be comforting to her. She had not realised just how good at it he was.

She drank more tea, sat up straight. 'I'm better now,' she said.

He stroked her hair for a moment longer, then took her hand, held it between his two. His grip was warm, and again comforting.

Suddenly it struck her. Toby was comforting her, and yet his home circumstances were much worse than hers. He had suddenly become guardian of a child he'd known nothing about, after a truly awful marriage. And his mother was very ill—in fact, dying of brain-stem cancer.

'Why can you be so nice to me when things at home for you are so much worse?' she asked.

He shrugged. 'You get used to anything in time.'

'Do you?'

His answer took quite a long time, and when eventually he spoke it, his voice was bleak. 'No.' he said. Then he shook his head. 'That wasn't very helpful, was it?' he asked. 'Annie, Caroline's death has upset you, but at least you'll come to accept it in time. And I think the state you're in is a bit to do with me. The past few days have been fraught for you. You've helped me so much that I'll never be able to repay you. Now I don't think you should be on your own this evening. So you will come to Carly's with me, won't you?'

'I'd love to,' she said. And she realised she meant it.

After that she felt a bit better. They chatted about anything but missed out medicine and families and their own relationship. Afterwards she couldn't remember a single thing that had been said. Occasionally there was a small shock of realization that she was sitting here with Toby in her flat, talking inconsequentially, just as if he were an ordinary friend. Next door was the bedroom where they had... And in that room, at the moment, was his child. Not her child, not their child, *his* child. At times it was a thought that was hard to bear.

But she was almost starting to feel better. And then, without knowing why, she found herself in tears again. Why?

'The hurt comes round time and time again doesn't it?' he asked gently. 'You think it's gone, you think you've conquered it, but then it springs up back.'

'Something like that,' she choked. She wondered if he knew that the pain she was feeling had two causes. One was the death of Caroline, The other was himself.

'You must be patient.' They were sitting side by side on his couch. He slid his arm round her neck, pulled her head down onto his shoulder. 'Just relax,' he said. 'Emotion makes you tired.'

So she half sat, half lay with her head on his shoulder and they said nothing for a while. And slowly she grew calmer. For a while anyway she was with Toby. Being comforted and reassured in his arms. And that was the only place she wanted to be right now.

CHAPTER SEVEN

TOBY drove into the parking space at the back of his flat, pulled in next to Annie's car. He switched off lights and engine and for a moment sat without moving. He could see light shining through the curtains of his flat. *His* flat. It seemed odd.

He had been to sit with his mother, just for an hour or so, and now it was as if he was a married man coming home to his wife and family. Annie had now moved in, bringing with her a bag of clothes, her books, other things she knew she'd need. She was keeping on her own flat but this was going to be more than a quick stay. He shook his head. He had never envisaged anything like this ever happening to him.

He let himself in. There were delicious cooking smells coming from the kitchen, He could hear Annie opening the fridge door, clattering pans. And in the corner of the living room his son, playing in his playpen. He went over to look.

'All well?' he called to Annie.

'Everything is fine,' she called back. 'Charlie's had

a bottle and we'll eat in about fifteen minutes. Would you like a mug of tea?'

'Please,' he said. He took off his jacket, scooped up Charlie and sat down in an armchair for a cuddle.

Annie brought over his tea. 'How was your mother?'

He shrugged. 'We all know she hasn't long to go. But she's in no pain. We think that she can possibly hear, understand what we're saying. So we talk to her. When I hold her hand she sometimes seems to squeeze it. And it seems as if she's trying to smile.'

'What do you talk about?'

'Family life. Holidays together. Sometimes I talk to her about my father. He died when I was eight but I remember him well.'

Annie's voice was quiet. 'Did you miss him?'

'I still do. But I suppose his death brought the rest of us together. We were…are…very close to my mother.'

'Yes, I know. I'm close to my parents.'

'I would have liked her to see or to hear Charlie. But we talked about it and decided not to say anything about him.'

'My parents would love a grandchild,' Annie said. 'They keep dropping hints. Now, chicken curry all right for you?'

'Wonderful,' said Toby and kissed Charlie on the forehead. He wondered if Annie's remark about her parents had been intended to be as pointed as it had felt.

Toby said he enjoyed her curry, and Annie noted he certainly ate enough of it! Afterwards he made her sit down while he stacked the dishes in the dishwasher. And then they had to pay attention to the little snorts and wails coming from Charlie, who was waking up. He would need feeding and then bathing.

Annie made his evening meal while Toby fetched the changing mat, the fresh clothes, the bowl of warm water. Then he picked up his son and held him on his knee. 'Going to have the same colour hair as your father,' he said. 'Like you, I was blond at first—but it went dark.'

Charlie gurgled that he was happy with this.

Eventually he was fed and bathed and put down to sleep. A job well done. 'Doesn't it take time?' Toby said, fondly stroking his son's head.

Having cleared away before, they went to sit in the living room, side by side on the couch, listening to the occasional contented gurgle coming through the baby monitor.

What should they do now? Annie wondered. What did ordinary couples do at this time? Not that they were an ordinary couple. They had been thrown together by circumstances and now had to find a way of living together.

'I could stay here and babysit,' she offered finally. 'If you'd like to go to the Red Lion or somewhere, have a drink with a few pals.'

'Thanks for the offer but I'd rather stay here. Do you want to go out?'

Annie shook her head. 'I'm happy here,' she half lied.

And so, like many couples in their situation, they turned on the television. This was just unreal, Annie felt. Were they playing at happy families or what?

Charlie woke up, they could hear his screams through the intercom. 'He's been moved about too much over the past few days, meeting a lot of new people,' Annie said. 'Even babies can feel unsettled. He just wants comfort.'

She went to pick him up, started to rock him. After a minute the screaming diminished a little—but didn't end completely. So Annie started to sing to him. Then she walked up and down, singing, rocking.

She could feel Toby watching her but deliberately didn't look at him. 'Shall I take him?' he asked after a while.

Annie shook her head. 'He's drifting off now. I'll go back into your room and put him down there.'

They had decided that whoever was going to look after the baby in the night should have him in their room. They would have alternate nights and tonight was going to be Toby's turn.

She stood in Toby's bedroom, glanced around curiously. He had tried to make it a bit of a home, as she had. There were photographs of his family—and one large one of him that she hadn't seen, of him in a white judo suit. He looked so—masculine in it. She sighed, carefully laid Charlie down.

'Haven't seen that picture of you in your judo suit,' she said when she returned to the living room.

He shrugged. 'You know I don't have much time for it any more. I used to be very keen and still keep my hand in now and then. But with Charlie I suppose I'll have to drop it completely now.'

'Don't give up anything until it's absolutely necessary,' she counselled. 'At the moment all you can see is the work. Your life will settle down after a while.'

And for want of anything else to do, she sat by him and watched television again.

Her sense of unreality grew even greater. Her entire life seemed different. She was watching television with Toby, not drinking with him in some bar, having a witty conversation. They weren't out somewhere, doing things. They were both tired so they weren't working. They were just together, but it seemed to her that they were together under false pretences. This should have been something that they both actively wanted, not something forced on them by circumstances. But reluctantly she had to admit it to herself. She was enjoying being with him.

She'd had a hard day and she was tired. 'Think I'll go to bed,' she said after a few minutes more. 'I'm getting myself a hot drink—want one?'

'Please. Want a shot of whisky in it?'

'Don't think so. I might get to like it too much.'

She made two hot milk drinks, brought him one. 'Goodnight, then, Toby. It's been a different kind of day, but we'll get used to it.'

''Night Annie.'

They looked at each other. She wondered if she should kiss him goodnight—just on the forehead, of course. She saw him obviously wondering the same thing, saw him starting to rise from his seat.

She didn't want him to kiss her! Well, she did. But she was not going to let him. Who knew what it might lead to? She turned quickly and went into her bedroom. It was only a small room and she wouldn't be in it very long, but she had tried to make it hers by bringing in photographs and a few personal items.

She finished her drink, went for her bath, laid out clothes for the morning. Then she climbed into bed. Outside she could hear Toby, deliberately moving quietly, he had turned off the television so as not to disturb her.

In the dark she decided she had enjoyed her first evening of domesticity. She had done little but it had made her happy. She remembered her own childhood, the certainties she had enjoyed. There had been rituals she had worked out with her own parents. She'd kissed both every night, and still did when she went home. Her dolls were safely waiting in a cupboard. Her child—if and when she had one—was going to feel the same happiness she had felt. She thought of Toby, was sure that he'd had a similar happy childhood. She knew his father had died early but she could still feel the great love he felt for his mother.

She turned the light off but although she was weary she couldn't sleep. Thoughts drummed around her head. She had been happy as a child. She felt that Toby had been happy as a child. Couldn't he feel it? That he, she and Charlie could be happy together? Maybe not.

Tears started to trickle down her cheeks. She heard the click of doors outside her room. Toby was going to bed.

After a while the tears stopped. She had told Toby she

would stay two months. She would stick to that but a lot could happen in two months. He might even see how happy they could be together. If he didn't recognise that happiness then they were no good for each other. That decision made, she could sleep.

Annie was in bed so he may as well go to bed himself. Toby entered his bedroom, looked down at his son. To one side was a table with everything that he might need in the night. Toby undressed quietly, made his way to the bathroom. When he came back the baby was grunting, making the noises that babies made. Of course he had heard babies before, on the wards, where there was usually someone else to deal with them. It was so different from having your own baby, one that was relying so completely on you for everything.

He was tired but, of course, he couldn't sleep. He thought about how his life had changed in just over a week. Now he almost felt married. Well, domesticated. And so, of course, he had to think about Annie.

He realised he had rather enjoyed his quiet evening with her, though he had not expected to. It was so different from the livelier nights he was used to. The time he had spent with his dying mother had made him rather low; coming back to Charlie and Annie had cheered him up.

He owed so much to Annie, how could he repay her? Of course, he knew what she wanted. She wanted a permanent relationship and, he had to admit, it seemed an attractive idea. But then he remembered how happy he had been with Gail. How certain he had been that it was something that was going to last for ever. He daren't risk another such happening. Apart from anything else, what would it do to Charlie?

Charlie woke up in the middle of the night. Toby tried just rocking the cot at first, but soon decided that this wasn't enough. He climbed out of bed, fed and cleaned Charlie, rocked him a while and then laid him back down. Charlie wasn't having that. He yelled again. Toby picked him up, remembered how Annie had calmed his child. Well, he could sing, too. Quietly he started.

Further down the corridor the lightly sleeping Annie heard the words. She came awake at once, knew what was happening. Should she go and help? No. But she wanted to, she was dressed quite decently in a long T-shirt and... No! She put her head under her pillow, clutched the sides round her. She would not think of Toby in his dressing-gown, in his bedroom, how grateful he might be and...

It was a while before she slept.

Next morning Charlie was going to the hospital crèche. Toby would take him. But he would have to be fed, bathed, dressed first. Annie and Toby got up an hour earlier than usual and even so only just had enough time. Toby shook his head as he carried his son to the car. 'Hard work, this being a parent,' he said.

They had told very few people but they knew the news would leak out in time. His family knew, of course, and

John Bennett, and she'd explained to Calvin, who would say nothing. But they were not going to hide anything. On the third day Toby had to be in hospital earlier than usual. Annie took Charlie to the crèche.

'Charlie, Toby's baby?' said Karen Frost, the sister in charge.

'I'm helping look after him,' said Annie. Exactly the truth.

'Right,' said Karen.

It was lunchtime before Eva said, 'Annie, what's all this about you and Toby having a baby?' Annie sighed. So, it was all over the hospital.

'Bit of a complex story,' Annie said 'I'll get Toby to come and tell you. But Charlie's not my baby.'

She found Toby in his room. 'I suspect the entire department wants to congratulate you on becoming a father,' she said. 'And they all wonder why the baby doesn't look like me. Have you got a story?'

He sighed. 'We'll just try the truth. But no one will believe it.'

The next three days followed the same pattern and then they had a couple of days off. And both of them were exhausted. Annie was looking forward to having more time in bed. She'd go in the afternoon if it was necessary.

Charlie had been put to bed; both she and Toby sat in their easy chairs. 'Tomorrow, even after he's had his breakfast, I'm going to lie in,' she told him. 'Just for a couple of precious hours.'

'I'm tempted to do the same. Did you say you were going out for the rest of the day?'

'Driving up to Lancaster to see my parents. Don't worry, I'll be back in plenty of time.' She looked at him and said, vaguely, as if it was a careless idea that had just come to her, 'You wouldn't like to come with me, would you? Bring Charlie and give him a bit of country air?'

It was an effort, trying to remain apparently casual.

He didn't answer, was obviously thinking about the idea. Finally, 'What would your mother say to you arriving with a man and a baby? Wouldn't she expect an explanation?'

'My mother would take it in her stride. She likes babies, she works in a school. And I'd explain how we are just friends.'

She could see he was intrigued by the idea and tried to convey by her attitude that she wasn't much bothered whether he was going to come or not. Though it was hard.

'I'd like to come,' he said eventually. 'It would be nice to meet them. But, Annie, are you sure this isn't going to make them uncomfortable?'

'You mean they might think that you are the man in my life? The true one, who will give them grandchildren? No. I've told them and I'll tell them again. We're just friends.'

'Then I'd like to come with you.'

'Good. Now I'm going to bed. Want the usual hot drink?'

It was her turn to have Charlie. She already had him in her bedroom, went to prepare the tray with the things she might need if he woke in the night. But he was getting better. A couple of nights now he had slept right through; she might have an undisturbed sleep. And she did.

They set off late next morning. There were things to do before they went—cleaning the flat, ordering more food, Toby had papers to deal with. And they both had to keep up with their studies.

Eventually they did get away into a day that was chilly but sunny. And Annie was enjoying herself. 'It's been too long since I've been out in the countryside,' she said. 'I've forgotten how good it feels.' She waved at the frost-covered moors to their right. 'Look at those. They're glorious.'

'Certainly are. I've not had much chance for walking myself recently, but I do love it. Annie, tell me a bit more about your parents. You know about my family.'

'Well, they'd both say that they're ordinary. But I think they're superb. They love each other and they love me. They always have and they always will.'

'Doesn't sound much to ask for, does it?' His voice was wistful. 'But it's not all that common. You say you are an only child?'

'Afraid so. My fault in a way. When I was being born my mother haemorrhaged and had to have a hysterectomy. But they would have liked to have more children, they would have liked three. Like your family, Toby.'

'Is that why you decided to specialise in O and G? Because you were an only child and you wanted to deal with children?'

'Perhaps. My parents both love children, they'd really like me to get married and present them with grandchildren. My cousin had a baby and she's gorgeous, but they would like a grandchild of their own.' Then she turned pink. She was looking forward to seeing her parents again, perhaps that made her a little careless about what she was saying. Would Toby take it as a hint?

Apparently not. 'I think that's great. 'I'm all in favour of three-generation families. Grandparents have a very important part to play.'

So she told him more. 'They've promised—or threatened—that when I do get married and have children, they'll move and live quite near me. There'll be constant babysitters.'

He smiled. 'So do you see it as a threat or a promise?'

'A promise. You know you're going to have to rely on Jack, Miranda and Carly a lot when I've gone. Then you'll know what I mean.'

'Of course,' he said neutrally.

They arrived just in time for lunch and Toby and her family seemed to get along at once. After lunch her mother insisted on feeding Charlie. Then they all sat in the living room, and the idea was that they would chat. But Annie couldn't help it. Her eyelids were going to close. And as she looked across at Toby, she saw he was in the same state. Then she looked at her mother and saw her laughing.

'I remember what having a baby was like.' Her mother smiled. 'I remember being tired all the time.

Now, why don't your father and I take Charlie for a walk, and you and Toby just sit here and sleep?'

'But I came here to see you and—'

'We just couldn't do that,' Toby agreed. Agreed sleepily.

'I suspect you don't have an option,' her mother said. 'You're both falling asleep. We'll be back in an hour.' And they were gone.

'If giving a guest what he really wants is true hospitality,' Toby suggested, 'then your mother is hospitable. I'm going to doze, I suggest you do the same.'

'Right,' Annie said after a moment.

Some time later she found herself in the kitchen with her mother, preparing a light tea, while Toby talked to her father in the living room. 'I like Toby,' her mother said. 'I always knew that you'd pick a nice man. Just as I did.'

'Ma, I haven't picked him. We're just friends and I'm helping him through an awkward time.' She looked at her mother thoughtfully. 'You haven't asked about him, have you? I'd have thought you were curious. Me turning up with a man whom I've no expectation of marrying.'

'Of course I'm curious, dear. But I've seen the two of you together, and seen the way you look at each other when you think the other isn't looking and I know—'

'Ma! You *don't* know.'

Her mother smiled. 'How many times have you told me that? And been proved wrong?'

CHAPTER EIGHT

ANNIE and Toby had a baby. No, it wasn't quite like that, they were sharing a baby. For a while. But although the baby took up many of their waking hours and most of their thoughts, they both still had jobs. And enjoyed them.

Four days later Annie was running a postnatal clinic, seeing a collection of babies and mothers who had been referred by health visitors, GPs or midwives, as needing perhaps more care than could be given by these professionals.

Her first case was quite serious, a baby with a recurrent chest infection. Why was it recurring? Annie arranged a referral for tests and an interview with the registrar.

Then something a bit more delicate. Mrs Thomas had asked to see a doctor, but specifically a woman doctor. Well, that wasn't too uncommon. When Annie asked how she could help her, Mrs Thomas blushed. She explained this was her first baby, it was all a bit of a shock, her husband was very good, but it was a bit of a shock to him, too. And carefully, tactfully, Annie managed to draw out what was really the matter.

'It's our sex life, Doctor. I don't seem to enjoy it as much as I used to. That is, we don't seem to enjoy it so much. I wondered if I'd changed at all...' Mrs Thomas went a deeper pink. 'Changed down there, that is. And I know he loves me, but if he's not enjoying it and I'm...'

Annie smiled reassuringly. 'Mrs Thomas, you won't have changed and what you describe is quite normal. You've got a new baby, you're both getting used to the idea. There's so much work, you're always tired. Both of you. Isn't that the truth?'

'Well, yes, I suppose it is.'

'And worrying over things like this only makes them worse. So that's the first thing. Don't worry. And then, when you're less tired and you feel like making love, make an occasion of it. Give yourself time, look forward to it. It'll all sort itself out in the end.'

They talked for another five minutes. And then Mrs Thomas went away looking a lot happier.

Annie fetched herself a glass of cold water, rubbed her tired eyes. She hadn't slept at all well last night, tormented by dreams of Toby. *I sorted that woman's problem out*, she thought glumly to herself. *Pity I can't sort out my own problem; it's just the opposite. Like Mrs Thomas, I'm tired all the time. But being near Toby all the time...the urge to touch him, kiss him, is almost more than I can bear.*

There was an intimacy living together, completely different from how it had been living with Calvin. Just yesterday she had just come home to Toby's flat, had been getting changed. She had been alone. She had needed to check something in her diary which she had left in her briefcase in the living room. So she had quickly darted into the living room, dressed only in her underwear. And Toby had walked in. They had just looked at each other. Each had seen the flare of passion in the other's eyes, had wanted to give way to it. But they hadn't. Both had stood poised, knowing that if he moved towards her, put his arms round her, kissed her, they'd be in her bedroom, in her bed, in seconds.

But he hadn't moved. Instead, he had defused the situation. A tiny, pointless joke. 'Surely the central heating isn't up that high?' And she'd managed to walk back to her bedroom with her dignity intact.

Who was the next patient? Annie looked at the list. Jenny Parsons. She'd seen the woman once before. Mrs Parsons was very chatty, had all the time in the world. She had a well-to-do but busy husband, a pleasant house, she didn't have to work.

Before Annie could even look at the baby, his mother took five minutes to detail what was wrong, what her worries were. She was a member of a new babies club, the other babies seemed to be doing so much better than little Joseph here, why wasn't he as big as the others?

Annie felt like telling her that it wasn't a competition. Joseph might be a little smaller than the norm but he was well within the parameters of what was acceptable.

Mrs Parsons sniffed. But she had been reassured, she was happy now. 'He's a lovely little boy,' she said. 'I don't know much about boys, of course. I suppose this bulge in his thigh is something to do with his…well, how boys are.'

'Bulge?' Annie asked. 'Let me see.' She looked, felt and she winced. Joseph should have been brought in much sooner.

'Right,' she said. 'I'm going to ask my colleague to look at this, if you don't mind.'

Mrs Parsons was instantly worried. 'Is he all right? Is there anything seriously wrong? Shall I phone his father?'

'I'm sure everything will be fine. Now, if you'll excuse me.' She reached for the phone. 'Dr Sinclair? If you've a minute I'd like your opinion. A lump in a little boy's groin.' She knew Toby had no patients at the moment.

Toby was there at once. He treated Mrs Parson to his comforting smile and she instantly calmed a little under his charm. He stroked the baby's face and said, 'You're a gorgeous little boy, aren't you? Now, what's this here?'

He looked at the lump, then felt the other side of the groin. He raised his eyebrows to Annie. 'I thought an inguinal hernia.' Annie said.

'I agree.'

'A hernia?' Mrs Parsons spluttered. 'Joseph can't have a hernia! Hernias are what old men get!'

Toby was good at explaining things. His voice calmed people, made them confident that he knew what he was doing. 'All a hernia means is that some of the tissues in one part of the body have slipped to another part. In this case we think that some of the contents of the abdomen have slipped out of place Nearly ten per cent of boy babies have this situation. It's not serious—in fact, we can often gently massage the contents back into place.' Toby showed her how he was doing it.

'So do I have to do that?'

'I think not. The situation isn't dangerous but it needs correcting. We would recommend a very minor operation, and we'd recommend it soon.' Toby lifted the phone. 'Now, shall I arrange an interview with a more senior doctor? One of our registrars?'

That idea obviously pleased Mrs Parson. 'If you would,' she said.

After Mrs Parsons had gone, Toby looked at Annie and noted how tired she looked. 'You look like you might need a rest. Are you overdoing it, looking after Charlie?'

'No, Toby, I am not. Just the opposite. He's a lovely little boy and I look forward to seeing him every night and every morning. It's hard work but it calms me.'

Toby pursed his lips. 'You know, he'll miss you when you go.'

'True. And I'll miss him.'

'Well, better get on with work.' And Toby was gone.

Annie shivered. 'When you go.' The words were like cold water thrown in her face. But then she remembered how seriously she had told him that she was going after two months. He was only sticking to what she had told him. He was being fair. But she had hoped that he would find that he just couldn't be without her. It was nothing to do with Charlie; he must want her for herself. Annie felt lost. On impulse she phoned Miranda.

'Love to have lunch with you.' Miranda said. 'Canteen in twenty minutes?'

'We've been together for three weeks now,' Annie told her friend as they sat down at an empty table. 'We're like an old married couple, slipping into each other's ways. I know what he likes to eat. He knows what I like to watch on TV.'

'Sounds good. How're you getting on with Charlie?'

'He's great, he's a lot less work now than he used to be. We know what he likes.' Annie sighed. ' Miranda, we're a good couple together.'

'Sex?' Miranda asked bluntly. 'I'll believe you if you say none, even though I'm the only one in the hospital who would do so.'

'No sex. This isn't a real relationship.'

'So how do you cope?'

'With difficulty. Sometimes, when we're tired, sitting together at the end of a hard day, I think how lovely it would be just to go to bed with him, sleep with his arms round me. And sometimes, when we're not tired, the tension between us is so strong you can feel it humming in the air. I know what he's thinking when he looks at me. And he knows that I know, and he knows that I want the same thing.'

Annie ate a mouthful of her salad and went on, 'Once or twice he's got up from his chair and I've thought that he's going to come over and grab me and kiss me and to hell with everything. And I've been half fearful and half hoping and I know I'm going to give way. And then he goes to look at Charlie or get a book or something. And I'm disappointed.'

'And a bit relieved?'

Annie sighed. 'I suppose I am. But then two minutes later he'll brush against me, just accidentally, and the touch of him burns like fire.'

'So why not give way? Make a definite decision that this is something that you want. Go for it, enjoy it and to hell with the consequences.'

Annie smiled. 'I have been tempted. But I don't just want sex with him. I want him to love me. I'm not asking him to marry me, just to love me and carry on seeing me and be aware that perhaps we could develop a relationship that could be permanent. But he's still terrified of making the same mistake that he made with Gail.'

'He should have more sense,' Miranda said bluntly. 'So what's your plan?'

'I've got another five weeks and I'm hoping that maybe something might happen. If not, I'm going to cut my losses and go to America.'

'I don't want you to go,' said Miranda. 'You're going to be my chief bridesmaid.' She thought a minute. 'Do you want…? Do you think…? Should I ask Jack to talk to him? Or even Carly? Carly has a lot of sense and is less combative than Jack.'

Annie shook her head. 'Don't ask either of them. You know the Sinclairs. They aren't easily pushed.'

'True,' said Miranda. 'So there's not much you can do but hope, is there?'

'Afraid not.'

'Like to come with Charlie and me on a mystery tour?' Toby said two days later.

'Sounds fun. I like mysteries.'

Right, then, I've checked out our shifts. We can both get away at four today. We'll pick Charlie up from the crèche. He needs to be mystified, too.'

'What sort of mystery tour Toby?' She was intrigued.

'A mysterious mystery tour. I guarantee satisfaction. Be ready at four.'

In fact, he took her to see a flat. And she thought it was wonderful.

They had been to look at a few flats, a few houses. They didn't have time for serious house hunting, and what they had seen had been—well, one or two places had been all right. But no better than that. 'Strange how your point of view changes when you're looking for somewhere more or less permanent, isn't it?' Toby had asked.

There was something intimate about picking a flat together. She had supposed people spent weeks, months even, looking for the right place to live. And she wasn't going to live in it. This was to be Toby's home, with Charlie. It didn't really concern her. Still, Toby was obviously interested in what she had to say. Her view mattered. It made her feel as if she was one of two partners. No! She was just helping a friend who was flat hunting.

He took her to a tree-lined area about ten minutes drive from the hospital. Quite a few doctors and nurses lived here; it was both handy and pleasant. 'Good nursery and primary schools nearby,' said Toby. He had obviously done his homework.

The minute she got inside the flat she fell in love with it. It was at the rear of a small red-brick block. The first thing she saw in the living room were French windows that opened out to a small walled garden.

'The garden's private to the flat,' said Toby, follow-ing her glance. 'But you have to keep the grass cut.'

'Toby! You could cut that grass with a pair of scissors. But, look, the garden will get all the afternoon sun. And it'll be a wonderful place for Charlie.'

'I'll have to start thinking about things like that. Let's have a look at the rest of the place.'

Annie thought it would be ideal for a family with a small child. The kitchen opened straight onto a small dining area which led into the living room. Easy to keep an eye on a child while you were cooking. There were three bedrooms, one *en suite* and a large bathroom.

'What d'you think of it, Annie?'

'I think it's marvellous,' she told him. 'I doubt you could do better. Aren't people supposed to spend months looking for something like this?'

'They are. I'm glad you like it because I like it, too. Do you think you would be happy here?'

'It's a lovely flat, but I can't really answer that,' she

said calmly. *Because I won't be here with you. It'll be you and Charlie. Maybe a nanny. Not me.*

Not the right thing to say. Instead, 'It's not really my business but there's the old question that we all have to ask ourselves. Can you afford it?'

'No problem. I have a little bit saved up.' Toby wandered around, opening cupboards, running taps, peering in the kitchen range. Annie thought he was like a little boy with a new toy. Then she realised she felt exactly the same way.

'Lovely *en suite* bedroom,' Annie said. 'And all those built-in cupboards. You'll be happy there.'

'I doubt it. If I have a nanny living in, she'll want her own bathroom. This would be the best place for her.'

'Of course,' said Annie. 'Well, I hope you get it and you're happy here.'

Toby drove her back to his own, now quite poky-seeming flat. The flat they had seen was fine but he felt depressed. He had seen Annie's initial delight, and for a second had envisaged all three of them living there together. A family. Charlie, Annie and himself. But she'd made it very clear that she was not a part of his plans. And he had to remember that.

A week later and Annie was enjoying her rest.

Toby had told her that she was looking tired, that she needed a complete change. 'But I'm happy here with you and Charlie.'

'You may be happy with me and Charlie. But you're

also trying to study and hold down a full-time job as a doctor. And it's a lot to do.'

'But I can do it. You do.'

'I have to, you don't. Now, I've got the same two days off as you so there's no trouble that way. Jack and Miranda have offered to help with Charlie so I suggest that you go and stay a couple of nights with your parents. You'll come back so much brighter.'

And so she had accepted. She enjoyed being with her parents. They went for a couple of walks together, but mostly she just read and ate. It was what she needed, a change from the emotional conflict that she felt whenever she was with Toby.

One odd thing. Her mother never once questioned her about Toby. When Annie mentioned his name, or Charlie's, her mother smiled gently and moved on to something else. Most odd. As if her mother was serenely confident that all was well in the relationship. Well, perhaps she had accepted that there was nothing serious between them.

Six weeks had passed since Annie had moved in with Toby. In another two weeks, unless something drastic happened, Annie was going to leave. And her faint hope that Toby might realise what he would be missing was slowly dying.

A couple of hours before she was ready to go home, there was a phone call from a distressed-sounding Miranda. 'Have you heard from Toby, Annie?'

'No. Miranda, is anything wrong? With Toby, with Charlie?' She couldn't keep the panic out of her voice.

'They're both fine. Well, they're not ill. Annie, I'm at his mother's house now. Jack and Carly are here. Jack's just sent Toby home with Charlie. He said that Toby had done enough and if he stayed much long here he wouldn't be able to function as a doctor or a father.'

'Function? Why not?'

'Toby's mother is dying Annie. You know she had another relapse three weeks ago. She's only got days—hours perhaps—to live. Toby's been at the house with her the past two days. He's stayed up with her two nights. He's done more for her than any of us.'

'He didn't even tell me that she was ill! He sent me away. And I would have liked to help.'

'Toby can keep secrets. You know that.'

'Too right I do. Thanks for telling me, Miranda. I'll set off at once.'

'Toby needs you. Trouble is, he doesn't know it.'

Her parents seemed to think it was quite proper for her to set off a bit earlier. Annie explained about Toby's mother; her own mother nodded understandingly. Then, as Annie packed, she made sandwiches and handed the pack to her as she left. 'Enough there for you and Toby,' she said. 'Please, tell him we're both very sorry.'

'I will,' said Annie. 'Thanks, Ma.' Then she drove down to meet him.

It felt as if this was her home, she thought as she walked into his little flat. But it wasn't. Or it wouldn't be for much longer.

She found him sitting in the living room, looking down at the sleeping Charlie. 'Toby, I'm home. How are you?'

'I'm surviving,' he said. He was barefooted, dressed only in a creased pair of jeans and an ancient T-shirt. He looked tired, there were drawn lines round his eyes. He needed a shave, his hair was more unruly than ever— probably needed cutting. And then he smiled and she felt a great rush of emotion that she could just not describe. Whatever else he was, Toby was always gorgeous.

'Toby, I've just heard about your mother. Miranda phoned me. Why didn't you tell me she was so ill? I would have liked to stay here, perhaps help you.'

'You do enough for me, Annie. I didn't want to impose on you. In fact, that's one reason I wanted you to go away.'

She thought of telling him that she'd quite like to be imposed on, but then decided not to bother. First of all a quick look at Charlie. He was sleeping, looked peaceful. 'Has Charlie had his—' she started.

'Charlie has been looked after like a king. He's fine. Miranda will be a wonderful mother.'

'I'm sure she will. Toby, when did you last eat? Do you want a drink of any sort?'

'I'm not hungry or thirsty.' But he looked both.

'You've had a hard couple of days,' she said. 'You need to relax somehow, even if it doesn't seem possible.'

He was sitting again, leaning forward to look at Charlie. She decided this wasn't a normal situation and she could touch him if she wanted. Just as a doctor, of course. She walked behind him, stretched out her hands.

She hadn't touched him, not really, not since that time they'd gone to bed and—Stop thinking and concentrate!

She felt the muscles at the back of his neck. 'Toby, you're as tense as a drumskin! Now, just sit there, try to relax and don't think of anything in particular.'

She stood behind him, put her hands on the great trapezius muscle that ran from shoulders to neck. And pressed in her thumbs. He grimaced in pain.

'These muscles should be relaxed,' she told him. 'I'll just work on them for five minutes.'

She wasn't a qualified masseuse. But she had seen how quickly, how easily a massage could relax someone, how it could bring relief from pain. So she had asked a friendly masseuse to give her a demonstration, a few tips.

The muscles of his neck, shoulders, upper back were tight. She worked on them carefully, trying to promote the blood flow, trying to ease them back into relaxation. It was hard work! It felt as if she were wrestling with him. But slowly she began to feel a result.

And she could hear or feel his breathing. It slowed as she calmed him. 'That feels so good. Annie, is there no end to your talents?'

'You'll never know.'

It had just slipped out. She hadn't meant to say that. Still, it was said now. And it was the sad truth.

She finished her massage, came round the couch to sit next to him again. He rubbed his neck, shook his head. 'I feel so much better. What now?'

'I suspect food. My mother sent you some sandwiches and I'll make you some tea. Just sit there.'

He did as she'd suggested. She ate sandwiches and drank tea with him and he appeared to relax even more. And then he started to talk. She wasn't sure whether he was talking to her or talking to himself.

'I've spent a lot of time just holding my mother's hand,' he said. 'She hasn't said anything much for quite a while now, but she lies there and I think she can hear. I hope she can understand. I really wanted to tell her about my child. But I couldn't, could I? Not at this late stage. So I rambled on about the past and about our holidays and I hope she heard me. And perhaps in time I—'

His phone rang. He didn't move, just looked at it. The phone rang again. He continued to stare at it then turned to look at Annie. 'Only one call I'm expecting tonight,' he said. And he lifted the receiver.

'Hi, Jack.' He listened. 'OK. Well, I'm glad about that… I'll come straight round and…if you're sure…' There was a longer break then, and Annie saw him listening intently. 'It was what we knew would happen but it's still hard. Love to Carly, Jack, oh, and love to you, too.' He replaced the receiver.

'My mother has just died,' he said calmly to Annie.

Annie lay awake long after they had gone to bed. She had moved Charlie into her room to let Toby sleep, and the flat was quiet. Unable to sleep, she got up and went into the kitchen to make herself a drink. It was then that she heard sobbing. Toby.

Quietly she tiptoed into his room. Having never seen him like this before, it broke her heart. Wanting to comfort him, to absorb some of his pain, she sat on his bed and wrapped her arms around him.

As she held him, she could feel the muscles underneath his thin T-shirt, could feel his body start to relax. And there was his smell—part Toby, part the shampoo in his hair, part the masculine scented soap he had used. And the tiniest smell of baby. She lifted her hand, ran it through his hair. It was good to feel it running through her fingers.

What was happening? Suddenly there seemed to be too much of him, as if he had grown. No matter how hard she hugged him, she couldn't somehow get all of him. His hands were resting gently on her shoulders, it was she who was pulling him to her. And then he kissed her.

His arms tightened round her as their bodies pressed together, and she could feel his need for her, hard and urgent. She knew he wanted her now. And she knew she wanted him.

She took her arms from round him, moved back slightly. He released her at once, but she thought she heard him sigh as he did so. 'Toby, is this what you want?'

He shook his head as if puzzled. 'I don't want to hurt you. I think I've done you enough damage. But I do want you! I want you in my bed, I want you desperately. But, Annie, that isn't the commitment that you want, that you deserve. I'm thinking of myself, of the comfort I'd find in your arms. I'm not thinking of you. And I should. '

They were so close together and yet not touching.

She knew that according to his own values he was an honourable man and so she knew that no way would he touch her again unless she made it clear that that was what she wanted.

She thought. She knew that what she was considering was absolute madness, that she would probably regret it for months to come. And she couldn't decide if she was doing this to bring comfort to a friend or to serve her own desperate needs.

She did it so seldom. But there were times when it was good to be reckless.

Very calmly, she told him, 'We had something together once and that isn't coming back. I accept that. But if we can just have one time together, totally without commitment on either side, then that's what I want. Just once, Toby. And you know I mean that. Don't you?'

'Yes, I know you mean it,' he whispered.

They stayed in silence for a second longer. Then he reached for her, and Annie knew she had made the right decision.

He kissed her, his strong arms holding her to him, making her feel the length of his body, his now more than obvious urgency thrusting against her thigh. And she revelled in his need for her, knew that he had a hunger that only she could slake. A hunger that she shared.

The kiss lasted for seconds, hours, who could tell? Then slowly, deliberately he eased off her dressing-gown and slid her nightie over her head. The garments were cast aside. Then she moaned as he bent his head to kiss each breast, flick his tongue against each firm upright nipple. This was too much!

For a moment again they gazed at each other and she could see the passion burning in his eyes, even hear the depth of his breathing. Then he turned to pull off his T-shirt and boxers, tossing them carelessly aside. Now they were both naked. She felt entirely happy, entirely unashamed. This all was for Toby. And she gloried in the fire that she could see in his eyes.

She reached for his shoulders, pulled him on top of her. 'Now Toby,' she panted. 'I can't wait. Please, Toby, now, I want you now.'

He reacted to her desperation, obviously feeling the same himself. 'Yes, now,' he muttered. 'Yes, I want you, too, sweetheart.'

Then he stiffened, moved away from her. 'Toby, what's wrong?'

He swung off the bed. 'Something I need,' he said, 'something we both need.'

He felt for his wallet, took something from it and there was the soft crackle of paper.

Good Lord, she'd completely forgotten! Thank goodness Toby hadn't.

It only took seconds and he was back with her. No, he was back on her. One last long tormenting kiss and his body slowly, easily slid into hers. She shut her eyes in ecstasy, feeling a sense of completion, feeling that now truly they were together. 'Oh, Toby,' she whispered. 'Now, please, now.'

Both were too far gone to hold back now. He plunged

deeper into her, gathered her to him; she felt his body in hers, next to hers, around hers, they were as one. And they moved together in a harmony, to a crescendo that would not be halted. She felt her world melting, felt that there was nowhere but here and nothing but the two of them. Fused together as one.

They lay there, panting, happy. Then she pulled the bedclothes over them, switched out the bedside light. He gathered her into his arms and for a while they both slept. An hour or two later Annie woke up and saw that Toby was awake, too. So they sat up in bed together and talked about his mother.

'It's no shock, you know we were expecting it,' Toby said quietly. 'I offered to go round and help with arrangements and so on, but Jack said if I insisted on going in to work he'd rather have me fit at the clinic tomorrow.'

Annie was horrified. 'You're going in to work?'

'I'm needed there.'

'Toby, you've just lost your mother. Is going to work really what you should be doing?'

'I deal with things my own way.'

Annie sighed. 'You don't deal with things, you repress them.'

'It's the way I learned to cope.'

She shook her head. 'You didn't learn how to cope, Toby. You learned how to push all emotion away, to feel nothing. You're not a person, you're a robot. You're a robot with a big smile painted on your face. Tonight was the first time I've ever seen human emotion from you.'

For a moment she thought she had got through to him.

There was just a flicker of reaction in his face, but then it was blank again, with just that irritating half-smile. 'I really do find emotions a bit too much trouble,' he said.

Annie stood. 'I'm not needed here. I'm going to my room,' she said. 'But before I do, Toby, let's get one thing straight. I've thought, hoped, recently that something might grow again between us. Foolish of me. I've learned more about you and it's all been a waste. Toby, I could never love a man like you.'

'Probably very wise of you,' he said.

CHAPTER NINE

THERE had to be a reconciliation of some sort. For a start there was Charlie to be thought of. She had made love to Toby of her own free will, knowing full well there was little chance of anything more happening between them. He needed her help, especially now. And she knew his mother's death was hitting him hard. So Annie decided that it was she who should make the first overtures. When she had calmed down.

Unable to stay in the flat, she decided to go out for an early morning walk. She couldn't sort out her thoughts, work out what she felt about Toby, what she should do next. With something of a shock she remembered her last words to him. 'I had thought that something might grow between us.' And 'I could never love a man like you.' Well, what she had wanted had been an open secret. He must have known. Still, perhaps for a while they could revert to their previous uneasy alliance.

She set off back towards his flat. And as she neared it, she had to admit to herself that it was no use. She and Toby would not get together. She should cut her losses.

In two weeks she'd get as far from Toby Sinclair as possible. And America would be ideal.

She'd made up her mind now—how did she feel? Clear-headed but miserable.

He was still sitting in the chair but now holding and rocking a quietly grizzling Charlie. She looked at them and her heart went out to them. And then she said, 'Toby, because of this and that, we're both a bit over-emotional now. Things were said that probably shouldn't have been said. I'm very sorry. Please, can we forget the complete conversation we had? Go back to just how we were before?'

Not a typical beaming Toby smile, but a sad, a wistful one. 'Probably a very good idea,' he said. 'And, Annie, you know, whatever I say, I never want in any way to harm you. After my family you've shown me more kindness, more thought than anyone I've ever met.'

'That's hard to believe because, Toby, no matter what, you're a very loveable man. Now, shall we stop worrying about our feelings and see if that little lad would like anything for his breakfast?'

'He seems to be making indications that way,' Toby said.

She felt happy as they set about their customary tasks together. Just as she was getting Charlie's things together for crèche, the phone rang. She heard Toby take it, it was obviously for him. When she went back into the living room he said, 'That was John Bennett. He phoned to say that he was sorry to hear of my mother's death. He also said that under no circumstances was I to come anywhere near the hospital for the next three days. He said I'd have things on my mind, I'd be a danger to my patients.'

'Do you think you would be a danger to your patients?'

'I suppose it's possible,' he admitted. 'But I'd like to think that I was above such things.'

She sighed. 'Tony! Admit it! You're as human as the rest of us!'

'Perhaps,' he said.

The funeral was four days later. Annie had wanted to come but Toby had asked her if she'd mind staying at home and looking after Charlie. 'It's stupid, I know,' he said, 'but I don't want him to be in a crèche when his grandmother is being buried. I'd rather he was with someone who loved him.'

'Of course,' said Annie, her heart twisting, seeing yet again how Charlie had managed to touch Toby where she could not.

She was waiting for him when he came back from the funeral, looking impossibly handsome in his black suit and tie and pure white shirt. 'How was it?' she asked.

He shrugged. 'It was a funeral. And if a funeral can be a success, this one was one. Much of it was Carly's idea. She said that a funeral should be a celebration of a life, not the mourning of a death. So that's what we tried to have. We had assorted people giving little speeches about how they remembered my mother. Carly was very moving. She was crying but she was smiling. Even Jack's voice quavered a bit.'

There was silence for a few minutes more and then she said, 'I've seen all sorts of different sides to you in the last few weeks, Toby. I started off determined not to be affected by you. I'd got over you, the always cheerful, always casual Toby. Then, somehow, I found you to be a much more complex man than I had ever imagined. You could be thoughtful, sensitive. Above all, you could be hurt, you could feel pain. And now you seem to have come full circle. You're as cheerful, as casual as ever.'

'That's me,' he said. She wondered whether to believe him.

Two days later she was running an antenatal clinic. It was fun to be back at work. Other people's problems, other people's joys, they took her mind off herself. Which at the moment was no bad thing.

Having a child could be a tiresome business. There were a number of tests, checks, observations to make. But the psychological state of the mums was also very important. Much of Annie's time was spent counselling, advising what was desirable, what was possible, what was actually bad.

'But, Doctor, I've smoked all my life. I need it. I've tried but I just can't give it up.' Amy Jones, a single mum-to-be, had been determined to do the best she could for her unborn child. But she genuinely could not stop smoking.

'You've tried the patches, the chewing gum?'

'Tried them both, they did nothing much for me but gave me a headache.'

Annie sighed. 'Well, I can't force you to stop smoking, Amy, but I've got to tell you that you're putting your baby at risk. Look, there's one last thing to try. Would you be willing to go to the anti-smoking clinic?'

Amy's time to sigh. 'I'll try anything once.'

So Annie arranged an appointment and hoped it would do some good.

Other appointments were different. There were women who were overjoyed, apprehensive but excited, bringing details of crèches and baby clothes and the choice of names. 'It's either Matthew after my father or Peter after my husband's father.'

'Both good names.' Annie had learned to be diplomatic.

'Of course, it might turn out to be a girl. And we just can't decide on anything.'

These were the kinks of things Annie had to deal with. And she enjoyed doing what she could.

Then, right at the end of her list, came Mrs Kent. She was slightly older than most of the mums that day and came in looking deeply worried.

'My husband I and have been trying for a baby for two years now,' she said. 'We were thinking of…of going to a specialist clinic, but then I fell pregnant naturally, and we were both delighted.'

'Good. Now, how long have you been pregnant?'

'We worked it out as seven weeks now.'

'I'm pleased for you. But if everything is going well, you don't need to see me for another four weeks.'

There was a silence. Then Mrs Kent said, 'I had a

period three days ago. I didn't tell my husband. I didn't take one of those tests you get from the chemist's. I just took things easy and made an appointment to see you.'

One of the hard things to deal with. Especially with an older woman who had been trying for so long. But there was no getting round the facts. 'Mrs Kent, roughly twenty-five per cent of mothers lose their babies in the first few weeks after conception. Sometimes it's nature's way of saying that things aren't going right. Sometimes it just happens—no one knows why. It certainly doesn't mean that you can't go on to try again. But the first thing to do is to find out for certain whether you are pregnant or not.'

Annie took the kit from a drawer. 'There's a ladies' right across the hall. I need a mid-flow specimen of urine on this stick. Go and get one and then bring it straight back to me.'

Mrs Kent did as she was told. And she and Annie looked at the little window on the stick. The result was certain; Mrs Kent was not pregnant. She sat there and wept silently.

There was not much Annie could do but comfort her. And eventually she sent Mrs Kent away, telling her to try again. And if she was not successful after a few months, to come back. It would be possible to arrange a visit to a fertility clinic.

A typical afternoon in the clinic.

Annie gathered up her notes and went to the staff lounge. There was paperwork that had to be finished before she went home.

Toby was in the lounge, also working his way through a set of notes. Right now he was not the person she wanted to see. She wanted to be quiet and left alone.

'We've both got to work,' she said. 'Let's make a pact to keep quiet until we've both finished.'

He appeared surprised at that. But he merely smiled and said, 'Whatever you want, Annie.'

And he was silent. But for some reason Annie just could not work. All she could see was Mrs Kent's face as she'd left her room. Annie wriggled in her chair, toyed with her papers, dropped some on the floor, cursed quietly to herself when she realised she had been filling in the wrong columns on one of her forms. After twenty minutes she had achieved nothing. And Toby had noticed.

'You're not good,' he said. 'I can make you a drink or help you with your work or you can just shout at me. But something is wrong. Is it me? A worrying case this afternoon? Come on, we can talk to each other about things like this.'

So she told him of Mrs Kent and he nodded understandingly. 'It must be hard to have something you wished for so fervently just taken away from you. But you know very well that not everything is lost for Mrs Kent. You say there's nothing apparently wrong organically. She can just try again and she'll probably succeed.'

'But I feel for her! Some cases you just do.'

She could tell he was trying to calm her. 'I know. But you've had a rough ride over the past few days, perhaps you're just a bit over-emotional. That's why you're so sympathetic with Mrs Kent.'

Annie sighed. 'Guess so,' she said. 'Who'd be a doctor with an excess of emotions?'

Toby was first home that evening. Annie phoned him as soon as he got home, her voice cool. 'Toby, can you manage without me for a couple of hours? I've got a few things to do.'

'No trouble at all. Anything important to do?'

'I've got my future to think of, Toby.'

He had a bad feeling as she rang off.

He picked up Charlie and the moment he held his baby, kissed him firmly on the cheek, he felt better. There was a purpose to his life.

Charlie was fine. Perhaps now he should think about Annie. Think about the things that both of them had quietly acknowledged but never spoken about. That she had hoped he would come round to loving her.

He had been so busy with Charlie that he hadn't even thought about it. What should he do about Annie? Did he love her enough to marry her? He thought that perhaps he almost did. These past few weeks had been hard work, but bliss. Only one thing was missing. He wanted her to stay. Not for Charlie, but for him.

But marriage? Maybe they could compromise. If she wanted. He would ask her to stay on at the Dell Owen, not go to America. Not stay on at his flat either, that was an artificial situation, he couldn't fairly ask her to do that. But if she stayed—who knew how they both might feel in the next few months? It seemed a good plan. He'd suggest it to her.

She got back to the flat earlier than she had expected. Toby was feeding Charlie. She automatically got out the bath, moved into the now well-rehearsed evening plan.

'I thought you'd be later.' His voice was pleasant, concerned.

'I expected things to take longer but I was wrong.'

'Come on, Charlie! Just one more spoonful!' Toby managed to introduce the last of the dinner into Charlie's rather smeared mouth.

'Toby, next week can you manage without me for four days?'

He was obviously shocked but he rallied. 'I'm sure I can manage. I'll take the days off as leave if necessary. Then he said, apparently casually, 'Any special reason?'

'I'll be flying to Chicago to look at this job I've been offered. I've just been to see John Bennett, told him that at the end of this rotation I'll be leaving. You know you've got hardly any time to find a nanny?'

This shock did get through to him. But he wouldn't admit it. 'Of course I know, I've had it in mind. I shall summon a dozen of them and interview them one by one.'

'Get Miranda to help you,' Annie advised. 'She might have contacts.'

She could see that he was nerving himself to ask, but his voice still elaborately casual.' So you're definitely going to leave?'

'I went round to see Calvin. I'm to look round the hospital next week, there'll be a job offer, and then I'll start in about five weeks.'

'You're moving fast.'

'If you've decided to move, you might as well move fast.'

'I had wondered…if I could persuade you to stay here for another six months. Do another rotation, it's very good teaching. We could see how things might develop…develop here.'

She knew what he was suggesting, had half anticipated it. But, still, what she had to say was hard. 'I don't want things to develop,' she said.

'You'll miss Charlie!'

It was almost a challenge and she had to be hard. 'Of course I will. But I can deal with the heartache. I've dealt with it before.'

'Of course you have. Well, this is interesting news. As soon as Charlie's settled, we'll open a bottle of wine to celebrate.' He smiled.

Typical Toby, she thought a little sadly. Never let your feelings show through. Keep up appearances, no matter what happens.

CHAPTER TEN

THE following Saturday she had free, and spent much of the day at her own flat, organising her clothes and books, throwing away what was not going to be used again, deciding on what to store and what to take with her. She was going to spend some time in America. She wanted to be organised well in advance. Besides, preparing for the trip made her more certain that it was the right thing to do.

Toby had taken Charlie to spend the day with Jack and Miranda. But he brought him back that night, and Annie had said that she'd be there at the usual time for the evening meal and bath.

She knew she was going to miss this. Right, she was going to miss it. Get over it and get on with her lift. Still...

'He's been a bit out of sorts all day,' Toby said. 'Grizzling, a bit lethargic.'

'Probably picked up a bug from somewhere,' Annie said. As she spoke, Charlie started to yell. She folded him over her arm and after a moment the yells diminished.

'He's quietening,' Toby said. 'We'll keep an eye on

him. Now. it's your turn to have him but would you like me to take him? He might wake in the night.'

'I'll take him,' said Annie. 'No point in altering the system.'

They had a quiet evening together, watching TV and reading. Both were perfectly polite but Annie had the feeling of something ending. And it made her sad. But she had made her choice.

She went to bed quite early. A quick glance at Charlie, he seemed pale but that was all. She read for a while and then turned off the light. She noticed that Toby was still up and wondered what he was doing.

It wasn't the best evening she had ever spent with him.

She woke in the middle of the night. A quick glance at her bedside clock, it was just past four o'clock. And Charlie was yelling. But it wasn't the normal scream of a baby who wanted something or was in mild discomfort. This was a high-pitched keening. Annie had heard it before and she shivered as she jumped out of bed. Charlie was in trouble and in considerable pain.

She looked down at him in his cot. He had been sick—violently sick. And when she touched his forehead she winced. His temperature was very high. She'd check it but even by touch she knew that things were serious.

Toby burst into the room without knocking. 'Annie…is he—?'

'Toby, he's ill. Come and look at him.'

Toby went straight to his son's side, while Annie

went to the kitchen to get a bowl of water to wash away the vomit. When she came back, Toby was sitting on the edge of her bed with Charlie on his knee. He was taking his temperature. 'Thirty-nine degrees,' he said. 'Annie, that is not good.'

'I know.' Annie took off Charlie's sleepsuit, sponged him down. Toby laid his little boy across his knees, gently touched that part of his abdomen known as McBurney's point. Charlie yelled even louder.

'I think it's appendicitis,' Toby said, 'I suspect it's quite advanced and the appendix might even have ruptured. So we've got the danger of peritonitis and...'

Annie saw the panic in his face. 'Toby, calm down! We've got to keep our heads clear. I agree with you but you don't diagnose your own child. You need someone detached. Let's get him to A and E and we'll have him admitted. Then the duty registrar will see him and—'

'We're both doctors we can admit him ourselves. Ring the night sister on the children's wards and tell her we're coming in. And I don't want the duty registrar. I'm going to phone Jack. He's the best paediatric surgeon there is. He might be a relation but I don't care.'

'Right,' said Annie. It might be cutting a few corners but it made sense. 'I'll phone the night sister, you phone Jack. Then we both get dressed.'

Fortunately she knew the sister on the children's wards and she was willing to prepare for Charlie's admittance at once. 'But I want another doctor admitting him! Not a parent. And don't worry, I'll get everything ready that might be needed.'

'It's in hand,' Annie told Toby. She dressed in seconds, found that he had done the same.

'Quicker to take him ourselves than go by ambulance,' he said. 'Let's go.'

She thought they had moved quickly. But Jack had moved even more quickly, and was waiting for them in the children's section, Miranda by his side. 'Put Charlie on that bench there,' he said. 'Now, quickly Toby, tell me what you've observed so far.'

Annie was surprised. Toby's account was brief, factual, unemotional. The diagnosis of a ruptured appendix was offered as a possibility. It was the perfect retelling of observations. Then Annie looked at Toby's face and understood. Only by being unemotional could he cope with what he had to say.

Jack nodded. 'I think I agree with your diagnosis. I further suspect that we might have peritonitis.'

He turned to the sister, who was standing by. 'Sister, I'd like Charlie here put on a saline drip. He's obviously dehydrated. He looked at Charlie broodingly. 'We could have tried massive doses of antibiotics if we'd caught this earlier. Caught this earlier! He's been in my house all day.'

Annie felt a range of emotions but said nothing. She suspected that Jack was suffering nearly as much as Toby. But he wouldn't show it.

'Jack,' Toby said, in what seemed to be an incredibly reasonable voice, 'if there has to be a laparotomy and a lavage of the peritoneum, I want you to do it.'

'In spite of my connection to the patient?'

'Yes. As parent I believe I have the right to nominate a surgeon.'

Annie hated the way they were talking about Charlie, as if he were just another patient, but she understood. This distancing was necessary if Jack was to operate.

Jack said, 'I'll operate if it's needed. Now, you two will go to the doctors' room with Miranda and wait. I don't want you cluttering up my work. Have a coffee or a sleep. And the minute I have anything to tell you, I'll do so. You are *not* to try and observe.'

'We won't,' Annie said. She took Toby's arm. 'And we're going to the doctors' room right now.'

Toby resisted a little at first, walking over for a last look at Charlie. Then Annie dragged at his arm and he came willingly enough.

They sat in the doctors' room. Miranda made them all tea; nobody drank it. For a while Annie tried to sit with her arm round Toby's shoulders but he sat perfectly still and seemed not even to notice it. So she moved it. Perhaps they could have talked, but no one appeared to have anything to say.

Annie could only guess at what Toby was feeling. For the first time in his life he was not able to rely on his own resources. There was nowhere he could hide, no joke he could make. In a sense, Toby was naked.

After perhaps half an hour there was a telephone message from the sister. The team had been assembled, Charlie was going to Theatre. And they sat, and after a while Annie made tea and somehow some of it was drunk. Toby sat still, staring in front of him, speaking only when spoken to and then in polite monosyllables. After a while Annie couldn't stand it any more. No matter how hard she tried to stop them, the tears came. Miranda came to sit next to her, pulled Annie's head down onto her shoulder.

Another hour and a half. And then the door was opened and there was Jack, still in his scrubs. His air of grim determination had gone. Now, he too, looked weary.

'The appendix was ruptured,' Jack said. 'I've tied it off, washed out the peritoneum with saline solution. What could be done I've done. He's being taken to the high dependency unit. Now it's up to Charlie.'

They all knew what he meant. In spite of powerful antibiotics, thirty per cent of children never recovered from a ruptured appendix. The next twenty-four hours would be crucial.

'I want to sit with him,' said Toby.

'Of course. Annie?'

Before she could speak, Miranda said, 'Annie'll come to look at Charlie for a minute. Then we're going to find her a bed here for the rest of the night. She'll need all her strength tomorrow.'

Annie thought about this. It seemed a good idea. The little party trooped down to High Dependency.

Of course, she'd been in High Dependency before. She knew what all the machines were, knew what they were monitoring. The machinery, the pipes and leads, didn't scare her at all. But when the tiny bundle in the middle of the cot was yours, things looked different.

Toby found a chair, placed it squarely by the cot and

sat on it. Miranda tugged Annie away, but before she went Annie put her arms round Toby and kissed him on the cheek. She didn't know if he even noticed.

There were bedrooms reserved near the ward for parents who stayed overnight to be near their children. One was found for Annie. She had a wash and tumbled into bed. For a moment she wondered. What would life be without Charlie? But, then, she was leaving him anyway. How would Toby cope if...? Toby would cope. He always had. Then she slept.

Next morning she went down to the high dependency unit. Toby was still there, still in the same position. By his side was a plate of biscuits, apparently untouched. There was also a mug of tea, now cold. 'We took him those in early this morning,' a nurse whispered. 'He just said thank you and then left them.'

'If you've time to fetch him another mug of tea, I'll make him drink it,' Annie promised.

She did. 'Toby you look dreadful,' she said firmly. 'You'll be no good to Charlie or anyone, feeling the way you must do. So drink this.'

He looked at her, slightly surprised, but then did as she told him. And a minute after that Jack came in. 'I want to examine Charlie and I want you two out of here while I do so. Annie, take him down to the canteen and get him some breakfast.'

She didn't do that. Instead, she took him to his flat, sent him to have a shave and a shower and then dress in clean clothes. Meanwhile, she would cook something for him. He was meek, did as she told him. Then he said, 'I'm going to phone Jack now. And then I'm going back.'

'Of course. Tell me what Jack says.'

Jack was guardedly optimistic. Things were going well so far. Good reason to hope, and the longer this kept up, the better Charlie's chances.

For the first time in over eighteen hours Toby managed to smile. 'I've been selfish,' he said. 'I've thought only of my own feelings and not of anyone else's. I know you have suffered, you love Charlie, too. You love him like he's your own son.'

And at long last Annie lost control. Perhaps because she knew that Charlie now was almost certainly out of danger. Toby would recover, was already recovering. And no one knew what she had been feeling.

'I do love Charlie. Not just because he's your son, and because I've got to love being with him, it's because I… Toby, I never told you, but once, I was pregnant…'

Then she gasped in horror. The silence in the room was almost tangible. Of all the things she had ever said, this was the one she wished she could take back. But it was too late.

'It happened to you? You mean you were pregnant and after a few weeks you miscarried?' She nodded. 'Annie, I'm so sorry, I didn't know.' She saw the concern, the caring in his face, the support she'd wished she had at the time, and it made her want to weep. 'So that would be why you were so upset after seeing Mrs Kent. When was this, Annie? Who was the—?'

'Let's forget it,' she said. 'I didn't mean to bring it

up. It was one of those things, an accident, not planned, it just happened. We did use contraception but…nothing is perfect. I was shocked, horrified at first, but then I decided to take things as they came and found myself almost looking forward to…to having a baby. '

Toby obviously didn't want to forget it. He persisted, 'And the man? The father?'

'He never knew. I never told him and very soon afterwards I finished with him. Which in many ways was a good thing. But I would have liked a baby.'

Toby was unusually quiet. 'You never told me this,' he said.

'Why should I? It's over. It's something I'm neither ashamed nor proud of, but it's definitely in the past.'

'And when was it?'

'Oh, some time ago. Three or four years ago, in fact.'

'Not, perhaps, five or six months ago?'

She had forgotten just how shrewd Toby could be. She stared at him and watched him cope with the idea and its consequences. 'Annie, I was the father! Wasn't I? You should have told me!'

She realised he had seen her stricken face, had worked out that he was the man in question. And now he was quietly angry. 'Didn't I have a right to know?'

'Toby, it was a casual affair. And it happened after you'd ended that casual affair.'

He leapt to his feet. 'No matter! I ought to have been told. You owed me that.'

'I didn't feel that I owed you anything. Just as you'd made it clear that you didn't owe me anything. We were over, finished, a pleasant memory, nothing more. And no way was I going to tell you after you'd ditched me. If things had carried on normally...'

'You mean if the baby had lived!'

'If the baby had lived,' she accepted calmly, 'then I would have told you. I accept your right to know.'

'But the baby died!'

'I've been through all this with Mrs Kent. It wasn't a baby. It was a clump of cells, that might, perhaps, have grown into a baby. People miscarry all the time, Toby, you know that. Now just accept it.'

'Have you accepted it?' Now his voice was cool.

'I thought it was something that might bind us together and no way did I want a man out of a sense of duty. So I did what I thought was the right thing, and didn't tell you.'

'You know how I feel about babies! My babies!'

'I do now. I didn't then.'

His shoulders slumped as he had to accept the force of her argument. 'But, Annie, you went through all that on your own. I would have been there for you if you'd asked. Annie, I'm here for you now.'

'Too late,' she told him.

'Right,' he said. And strode out of the room, leaving Annie staring after him.

Toby sat on his bed. His head was still reeling from what Annie had told him. They'd almost had a child. For a while she had known she was pregnant and had not told him. Because he had finished with her. A part of him could imagine her fear and her anger. And she had kept it all to herself! Hadn't she known him well enough to know he would have been supportive? Honesty made him admit that perhaps she hadn't known him that well—and that it was his fault because he had never let her get that close. So why was he so angry?

He knew she was right about one thing—about a quarter of all conceptions miscarried. Often the woman didn't even know she was pregnant. And she hadn't been carrying a baby, just a bundle of cells that might, that could have turned into a baby. He had no right to feel angry. So why did he?

When he came out of his bedroom Annie had gone. Toby walked back to the hospital.

He stayed by his son's side all day. But he felt confident enough to come home that night, having secured the firm promise from the night sister that if anything at all went wrong, she'd phone him.

Annie wasn't in his flat. All her possessions had been removed. He phoned her flat, but there was no answer. In desperation he went in search of Calvin, who told him that Annie was about to leave for America. 'She's just the kind of doctor the department is looking for,' Calvin enthused. 'Chances are, when they get her there, they won't even let her come back home. But she phoned them, apparently concerned about your young Charlie. They told her to come on a later plane.'

'So she's still in England?'

'Somewhere, yes.'

The next day Charlie was moved out of the high dependency unit and into Nightingale Ward. In a couple of days he might be moved into Kingfisher Ward. Jack told Toby that he couldn't guarantee a recovery, but this one looked reasonably certain.

And no one seemed to have seen Annie.

Calvin had told Toby that her plane to America was the next day. And Toby had a brainwave. He phoned Annie's parents.

Annie's mother seemed very pleased and quite unsurprised to hear from him. 'She's just set off back, dear. She has packing to do. If you go to her flat in, say, a couple of hours, you should find her. Will we be seeing the pair of you again soon?'

'I hope so,' said Toby.

Annie had decided to write Toby a letter. No need to see him, a clean break would be better that way. She had sneaked into Nightingale Ward, had a last look at Charlie. She didn't even have a photograph of him! She had sorted things out with John Bennett. She didn't even have to come back if she was offered a job at once. All she had to do was pack.

But she still knew who it would be when the doorbell rang. She thought about ignoring it. But she knew he'd never go away.

Of course, it was Toby. But a different Toby. His face was still tired, the way it had been the past few days. And his smile was uncertain, wondering. But he seemed pleased to see her.

'I couldn't let you go to get a new job without saying goodbye,' he said. 'So I came to meet you here.'

'How did you know I was here?'

'I rang your mother.'

Annie sighed. 'I was going to write you a letter. Leave without any more passion. I think I'm getting like you, Toby. Emotion just isn't worth the effort.'

'May I come in?'

She sighed again. 'I can't see much point. But yes.'

And then they were standing looking at each other in her living room. There were packing cases all over the floor.

'Is Charlie all right?' she asked. 'That's not why you're here?'

'Charlie is fine, I guess he's out of danger. Even Jack said so.'

'So what do you want?'

'I want you,' he said.

'Sorry? You know we arranged all this weeks ago. I'm going to Chicago for three days. I'm going to accept a job there and I might even stay. I'm sure you can get a nanny for Charlie a few days early.'

'I know.' He took her hands in his, pulled her closer to him. 'But I don't want you to go to America. Either now or for good in a few weeks.'

She gave a little gasp of annoyance. 'Toby, we've been through all this, made our decisions. I'm not coming back to mess about with you and—'

'I want you to stop messing around. Or being messed around. I don't want you back for Charlie either, although he'll miss you and I suspect you'll miss him.

You're the nearest he's got to having a real mother.' He shook his head. 'But this time I'm being selfish. I want you back for me.'

He seemed to have got even closer to her. His arms were round her, that face she so much loved was close to hers.

'You want me?' she asked cautiously. 'Just want me?'

'All right.' He paused a moment. 'Annie, I love you. If I'm honest, I've loved you for months. But I've been scared. I should have known better. Now I can tell you that what I'm feeling is more and better than anything else I've ever experienced before. I love you. I can't imagine loving anyone more than I love you and I don't want to lose you again.' He took a deep breath. 'Annie, will you marry me?'

She looked at him open-mouthed. 'Will I what?'

'Well, we've known each other for long enough. You know all my faults and I'd know all of yours if you had any. I like your family and you like mine. I want you to marry me. Not as a mother for Charlie—though that'll be wonderful—but as a wife for me. Annie, think about it. Do you love me? Perhaps I should have asked you that first.'

He looked at her anxiously.

'Love you? Toby Sinclair, you've put me through more heartache than anyone else in my life. The times I've cried into my pillow because of you. The times I've worried about you. The times I've spent wishing you could love me.' She stopped and then considered. 'Of course I love you. Why else would I put up with so much?'

Now they were pressed together and gently, oh, so gently, he kissed her on the lips. 'So you'll marry me?'

Annie smiled, seeing the love in her future husband's eyes and feeling overwhelmed with happiness. 'Of course I will. Let's go tell Charlie our good news.'

EPILOGUE

A LOT had happened in the past sixteen months, Annie thought. The happiest sixteen months of her life.

It was warm here in the afternoon sun, in the little garden in the back of the flat. The flat that they had chosen together. The place they were so happy in. They spent a lot of time out here. The three of them. Soon to be four.

Annie smiled as she passed her hand over her swollen belly, then smiled more as it kicked her. Not it! He or she. She had deliberately opted not to find out. Two months more and Charlie would have a brother or a sister.

She stood, walked cautiously over to where Charlie was playing. Charlie looked up, smiled. He placed his hand on the front of Annie's dress. 'Baby,' he said, carefully and proudly.

'Baby,' Annie agreed.

Toby came into the garden, carrying orange juice for all of them. Frosted glasses for himself and Annie, a plastic mug for Charlie.

'I've done it,' he said. 'I've phoned.'

Annie looked at him, a little concerned. 'How did it go?'

He looked thoughtful. 'It went well. Ursula was thrilled to hear her grandson is thriving. And she would like to visit. She even suggested that we come and visit her. She realises that she rather misses being a grandmother, and I reminded her that Charlie needs his grandmother, too.'

Annie nodded, pleased. 'So you'll think you'll get on, then?'

Toby grinned. 'I hope so. Anyway, she brought me Charlie, indirectly perhaps she brought me you. I'm probably her biggest fan. She ended up bringing me so much happiness.'

Annie smiled as he gave her a loving, gentle kiss. 'And me,' she said softly. 'More than I ever dreamed was possible.'

0207/03a

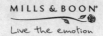

Live the emotion

Medical
romance™

THE SURGEON'S CHOSEN WIFE
by Fiona Lowe

GP and single mother Sarah Rigby is intrigued by her
new neighbour, hot-shot surgeon Ryan Harrison.
Sarah knows that Ryan is struggling to overcome the
effects of an accident, so she and her young son Sam
resolve to show Ryan how to live again. Soon Ryan
cannot deny his desire to be part of the family he
has grown to love...

A DOCTOR WORTH WAITING FOR
by Margaret McDonagh

Dr Conor Anderson was immediately intrigued
by locum Kate Fisher – she made him want to get
closer. As guarded as Kate was, she couldn't hide
that she was a passionate woman. But it was only a
matter of time before Kate's past would send her on
the run again... Could this playboy doctor finally be
the one to heal her?

HER L.A. KNIGHT by Lynne Marshall

China Seabury needs a host for her latest charity
event. and it looks as if she's going to have to grit
her teeth and ask for help from the Los Angeles
ER Department's infamous playboy, Dr Ric Morell.
Ric is delighted when China asks for his help, and is
determined to earn her trust – and to come to her
rescue in many other ways...

On sale 2nd March 2007

Available at WHSmith, Tesco, ASDA, and all good bookshops
www.millsandboon.co.uk

0207/25/MB071

From No. 1 *New York Times* bestselling author Nora Roberts

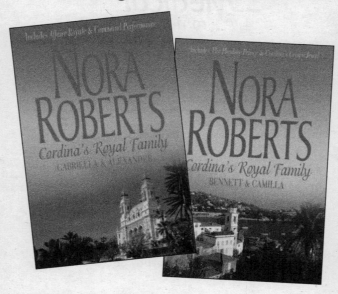

Romance and intrigue are woven together in these classic stories about Cordina's royal family

Gabriella & Alexander
Available 2nd February 2007

Bennett & Camilla
Available 4th May 2007

FREE

4 BOOKS AND A SURPRISE GIFT!

We would like to take this opportunity to thank you for reading this Mills & Boon® book by offering you the chance to take FOUR more specially selected titles from the Medical Romance™ series absolutely FREE! We're also making this offer to introduce you to the benefits of the Mills & Boon® Reader Service™—

- ★ **FREE home delivery**
- ★ **FREE gifts and competitions**
- ★ **FREE monthly Newsletter**
- ★ **Books available before they're in the shops**
- ★ **Exclusive Reader Service offers**

Accepting these FREE books and gift places you under no obligation to buy; you may cancel at any time, even after receiving your free shipment. Simply complete your details below and return the entire page to the address below. You don't even need a stamp!

YES! Please send me 4 free Medical Romance books and a surprise gift. I understand that unless you hear from me, I will receive 6 superb new titles every month for just £2.80 each, postage and packing free. I am under no obligation to purchase any books and may cancel my subscription at any time. The free books and gift will be mine to keep in any case.

M7ZEE

Ms/Mrs/Miss/Mr..Initials ....
BLOCK CAPITALS PLEASE

Surname ....

Address ....

....

....Postcode ....

Send this whole page to:
The Reader Service, FREEPOST CN81, Croydon, CR9 3WZ